THE MYSTICAL PENCIL

RAGING ROBOTS

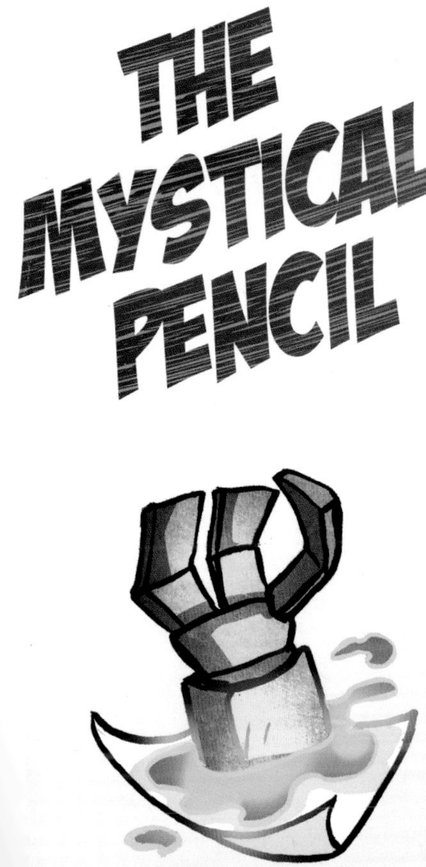

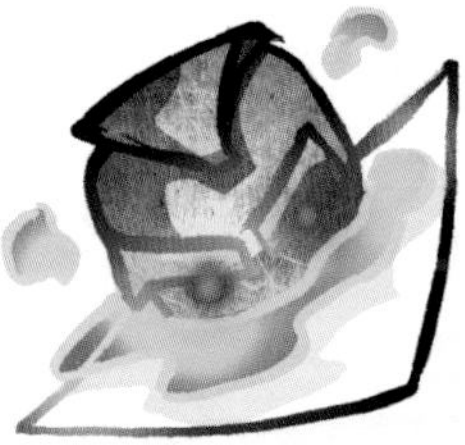

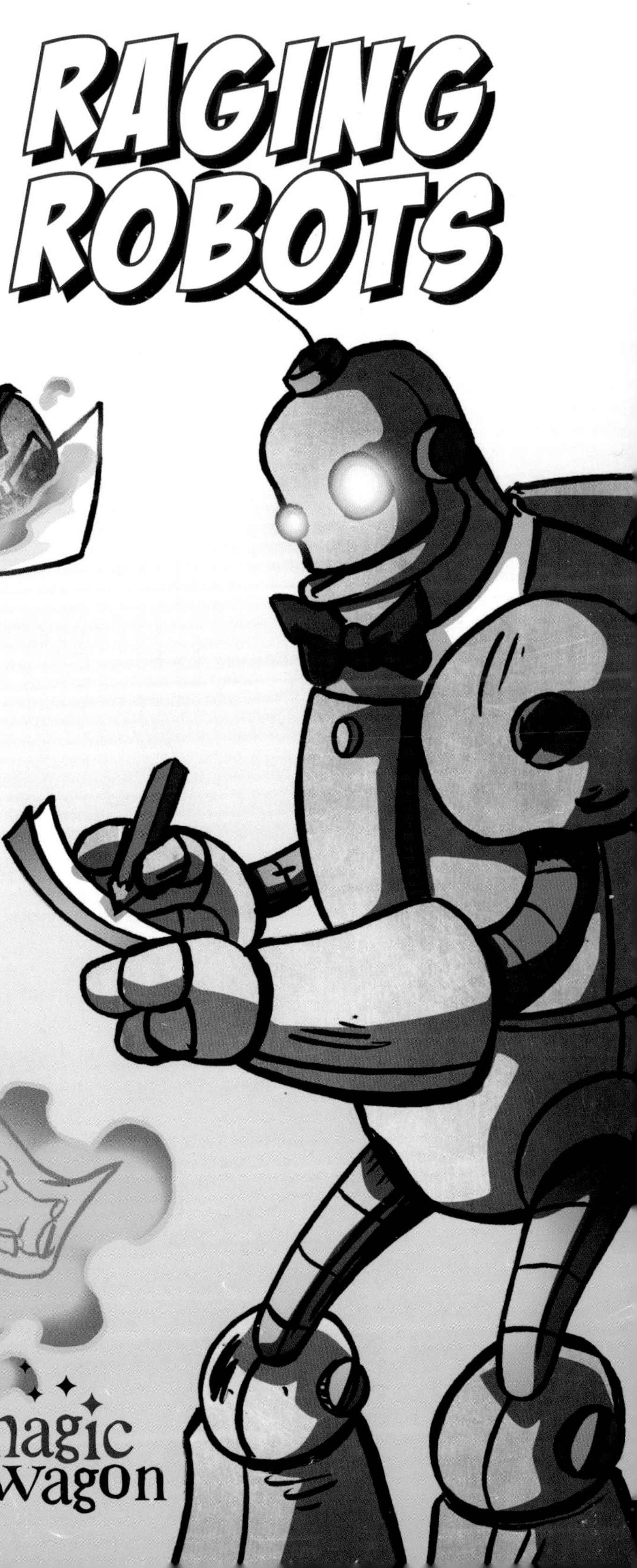

Written and Illustrated by
Dustin Evans

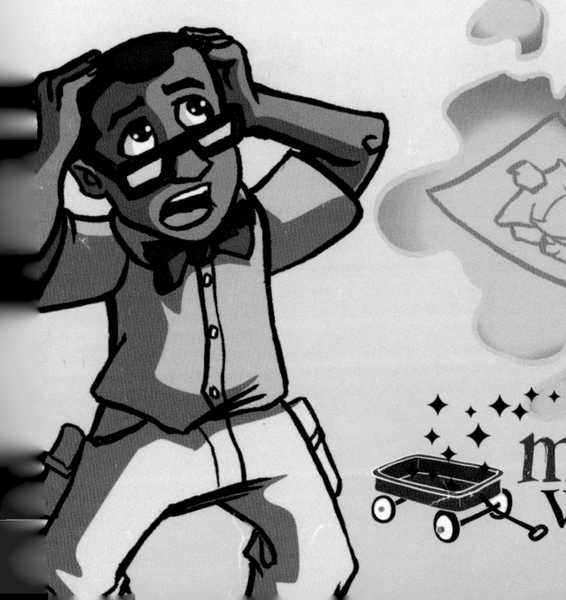

magic wagon

visit us at
www.abdopublishing.com

Published by Magic Wagon, a division of the ABDO Group, PO Box 398166, Minneapolis, MN
55439. Copyright © 2013 by Abdo Consulting Group, Inc. International copyrights reserved in
all countries. All rights reserved. No part of this book may be reproduced in any form without
written permission from the publisher.

Graphic Planet™ is a trademark and logo of Magic Wagon.

Printed in the United States of America, North Mankato, Minnesota.
102012
012013
This book contains at least 10% recycled materials.

Written and Illustrated by Dustin Evans
Edited by Stephanie Hedlund and Rochelle Baltzer
Cover art by Dustin Evans
Cover design by Neil Klinepier

Library of Congress Cataloging-in-Publication Data

Evans, Dustin, 1982-
  Raging robots / written & illustrated by Dustin Evans.
    p. cm. -- (The mystical pencil)
  Summary: Stewart has found the mystical pencil where Alex and Sara left it, and before they can
warn him he draws a robot that comes to life--and begins to use the pencil to draw other robots.
  ISBN 978-1-61641-929-5
1. Pencils--Comic books, strips, etc. 2. Pencils--Juvenile fiction. 3. Robots--Comic books,
strips, etc. 4. Robots--Juvenile fiction. 5. Imagination--Comic books, strips, etc. 6. Imagination-
-Juvenile fiction. 7. Graphic novels. [1. Graphic novels. 2. Pencils--Fiction. 3. Robots--Fiction. 4.
Imagination--Fiction.] I. Title.
  PZ7.7.E92Rag 2013
  741.5'973--dc23
                    2012027941

Contents

Previously in *Costume Craziness . . .*

Alex's dad returned from an archaeological dig and brought back many artifacts. When Alex needed a pencil to finish his project on the Renaissance time period, he got an old, beat-up one from his dad's bag.

That beat-up pencil didn't look like much, but it had great powers! The monster Alex drew suddenly came to life! Alex had to think quickly to make things right. He drew the morning as

if it were all a dream. He woke up to find everything was back to normal... but one thing was missing —the Mystical Pencil!

Sara had found the pencil on the street and brought it to school to draw costumes for the class play. Alex and Sara worked together to keep the farm creatures from turning the school into a pigpen!

When everything was back to normal, Sara tossed the pencil off the stage. And that's where Stewart found it. Its adventure continues here...

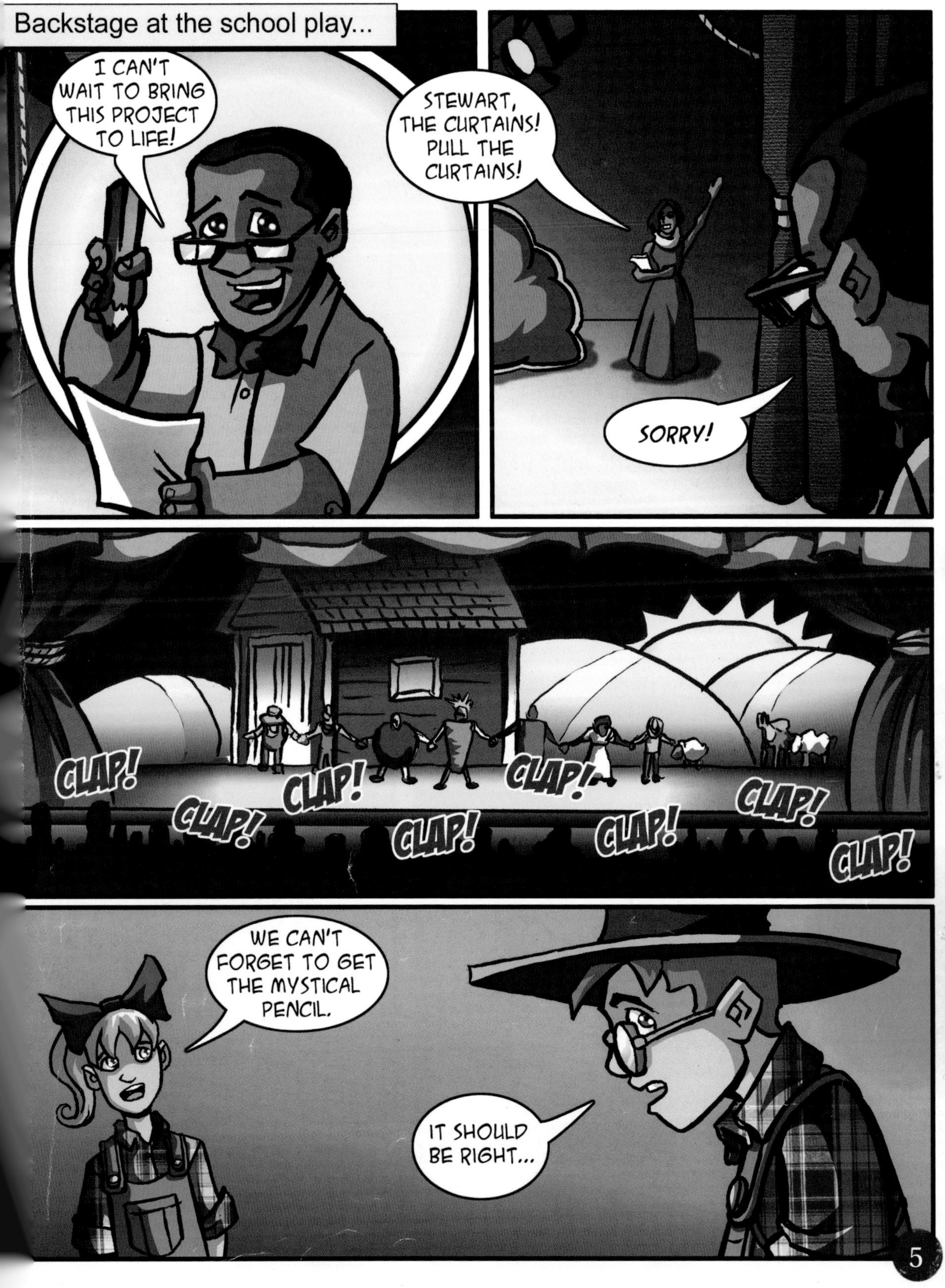
Backstage at the school play...
I CAN'T WAIT TO BRING THIS PROJECT TO LIFE!
STEWART, THE CURTAINS! PULL THE CURTAINS!
SORRY!
CLAP! CLAP! CLAP! CLAP! CLAP! CLAP! CLAP! CLAP!
WE CAN'T FORGET TO GET THE MYSTICAL PENCIL.
IT SHOULD BE RIGHT...

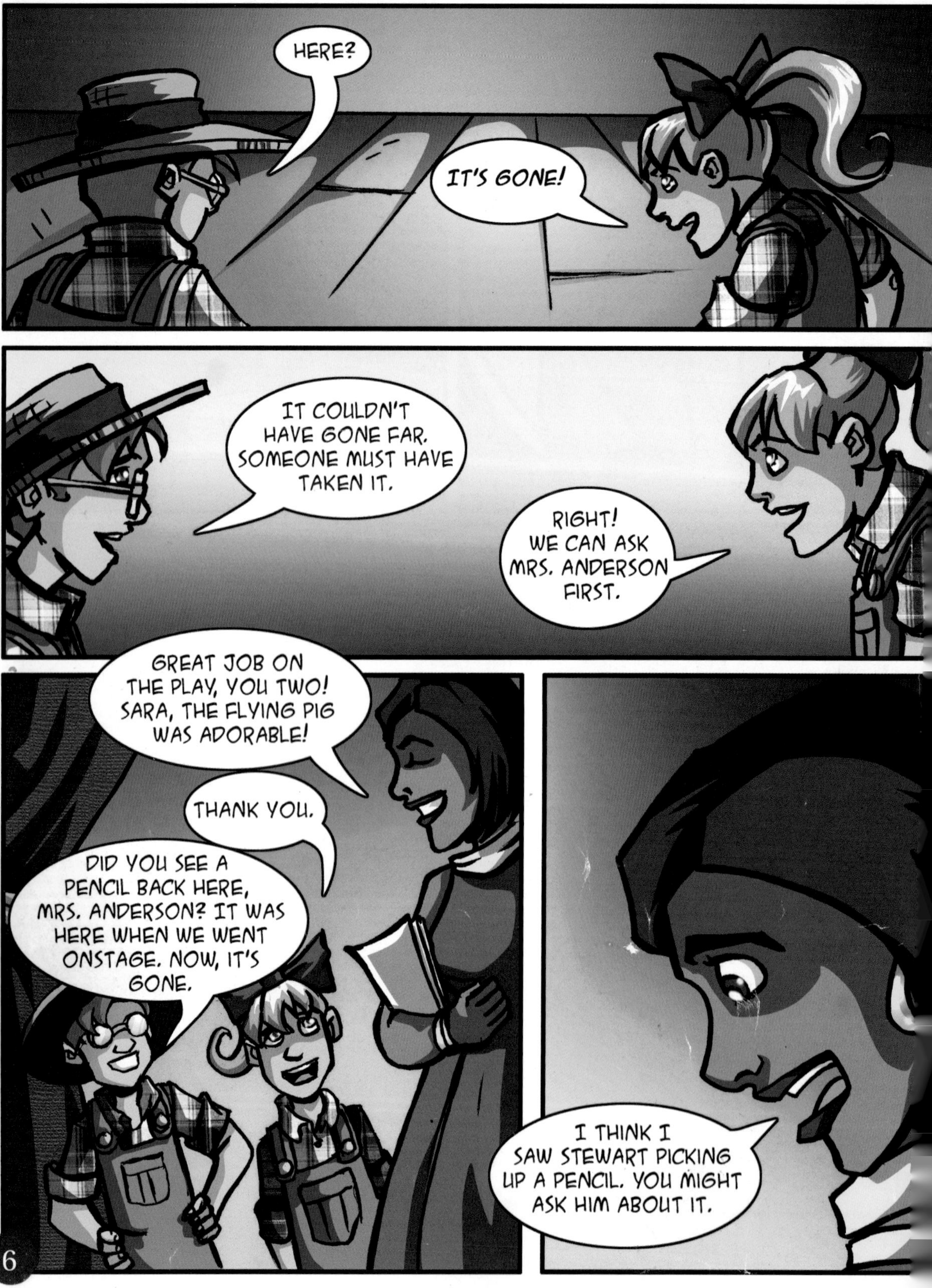
HERE?
IT'S GONE!
IT COULDN'T HAVE GONE FAR. SOMEONE MUST HAVE TAKEN IT.
RIGHT! WE CAN ASK MRS. ANDERSON FIRST.
GREAT JOB ON THE PLAY, YOU TWO! SARA, THE FLYING PIG WAS ADORABLE!
THANK YOU.
DID YOU SEE A PENCIL BACK HERE, MRS. ANDERSON? IT WAS HERE WHEN WE WENT ONSTAGE. NOW, IT'S GONE.
I THINK I SAW STEWART PICKING UP A PENCIL. YOU MIGHT ASK HIM ABOUT IT.

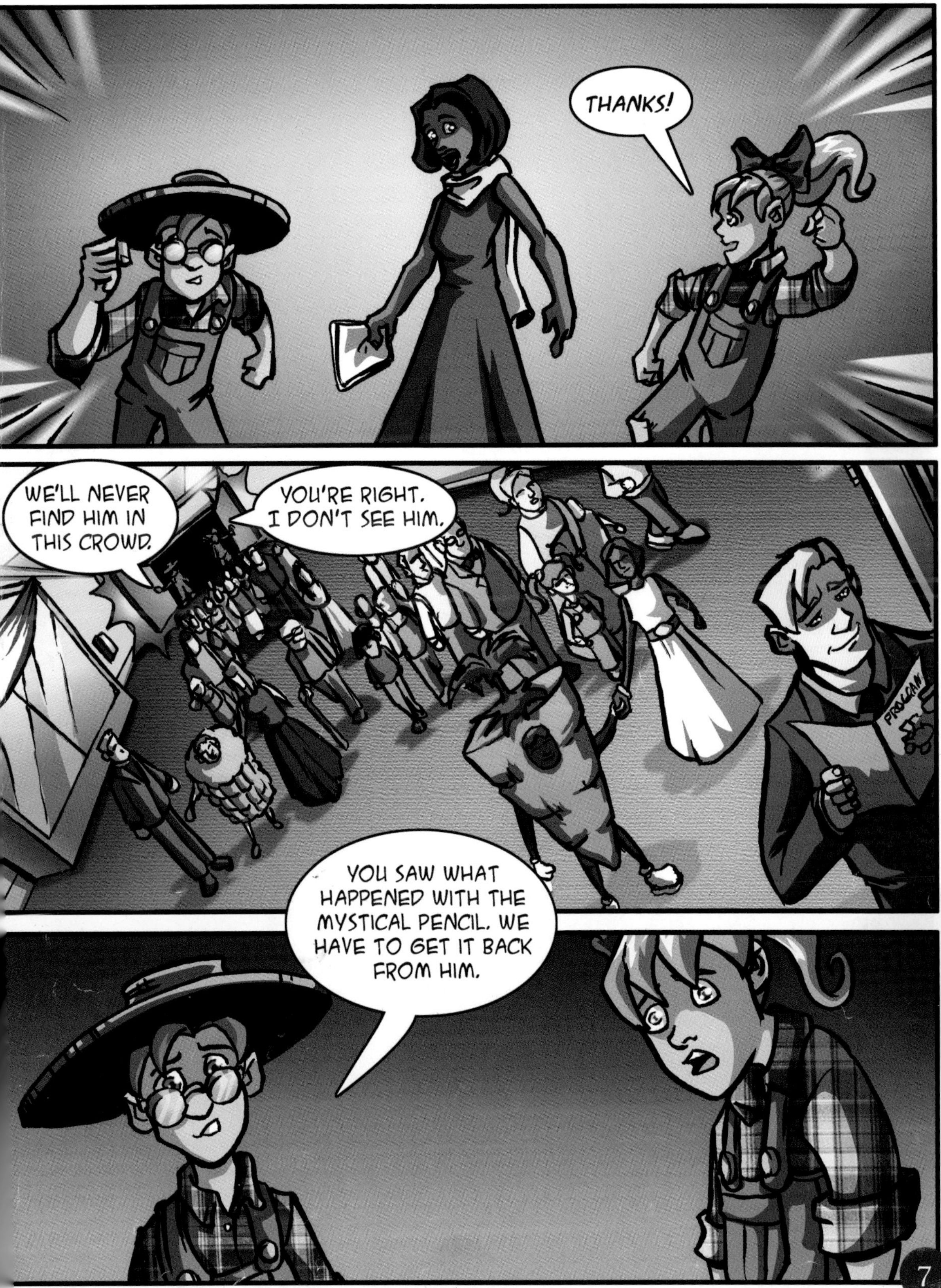

THANKS!
WE'LL NEVER FIND HIM IN THIS CROWD.
YOU'RE RIGHT. I DON'T SEE HIM.
PROGRAM
YOU SAW WHAT HAPPENED WITH THE MYSTICAL PENCIL. WE HAVE TO GET IT BACK FROM HIM.

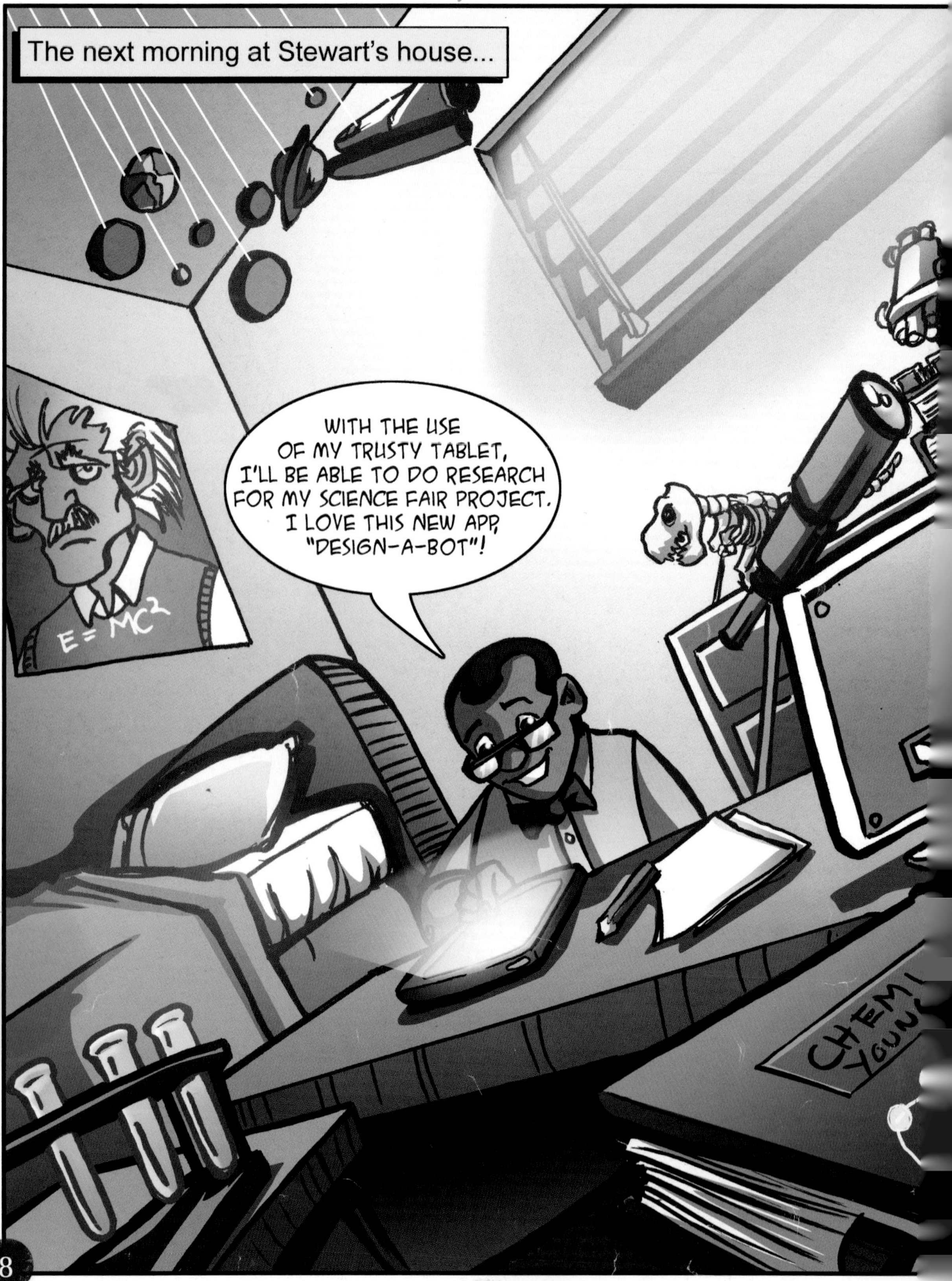
The next morning at Stewart's house...
WITH THE USE OF MY TRUSTY TABLET, I'LL BE ABLE TO DO RESEARCH FOR MY SCIENCE FAIR PROJECT. I LOVE THIS NEW APP, "DESIGN-A-BOT"!
E = MC2

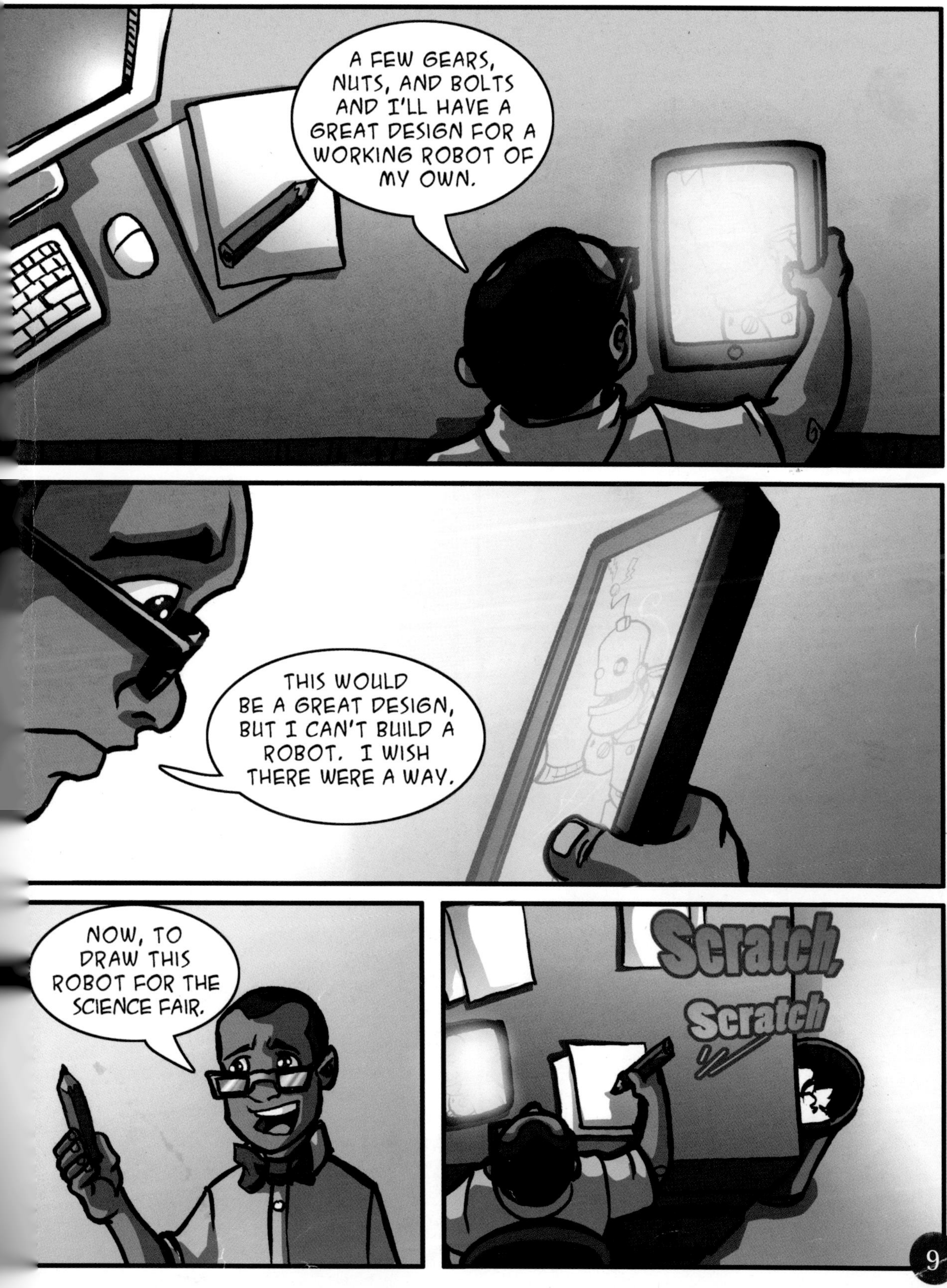
A FEW GEARS, NUTS, AND BOLTS AND I'LL HAVE A GREAT DESIGN FOR A WORKING ROBOT OF MY OWN.
THIS WOULD BE A GREAT DESIGN, BUT I CAN'T BUILD A ROBOT. I WISH THERE WERE A WAY.
NOW, TO DRAW THIS ROBOT FOR THE SCIENCE FAIR.
Scratch,
Scratch

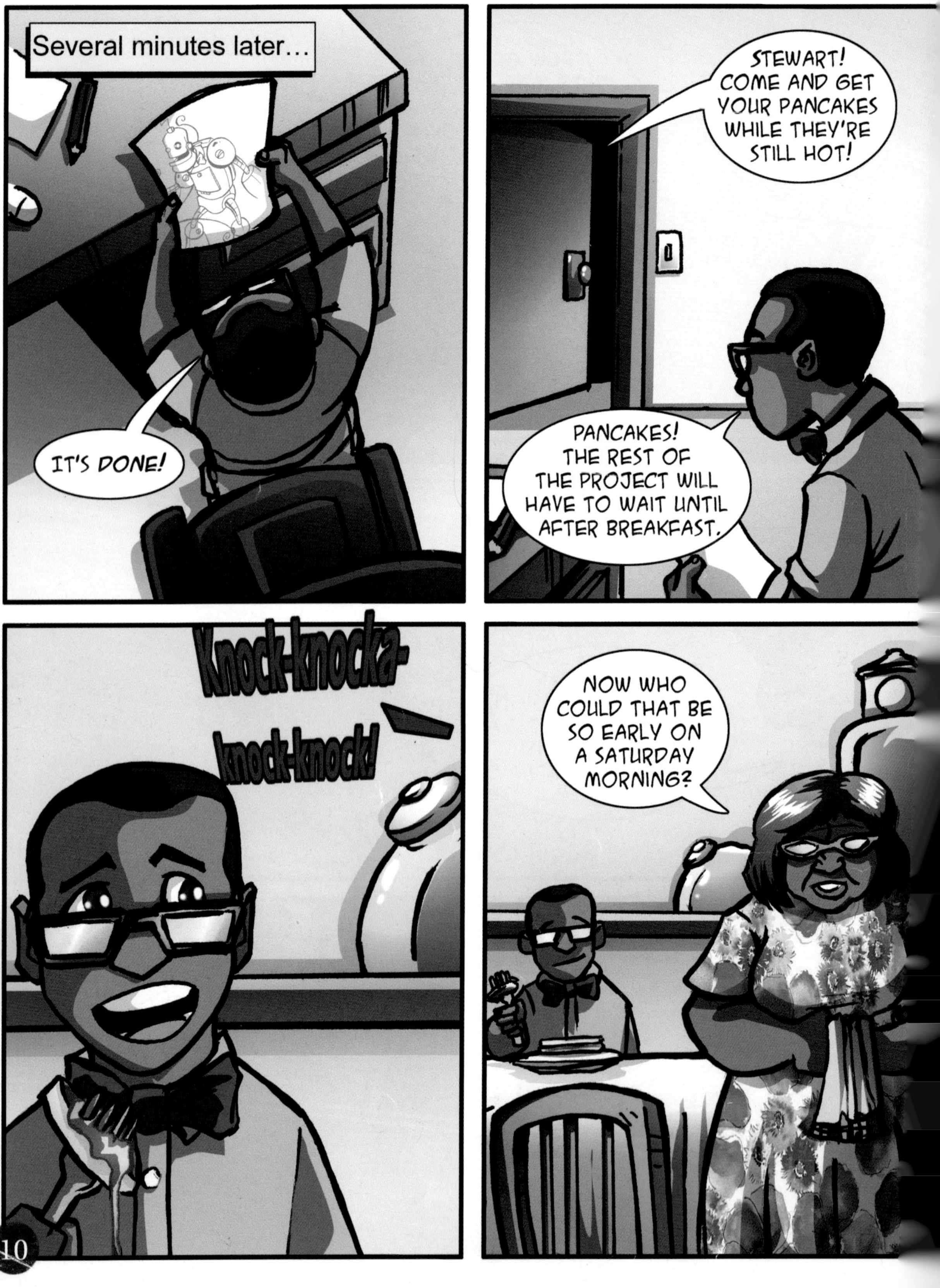
Several minutes later...
IT'S DONE!
STEWART! COME AND GET YOUR PANCAKES WHILE THEY'RE STILL HOT!
PANCAKES! THE REST OF THE PROJECT WILL HAVE TO WAIT UNTIL AFTER BREAKFAST.
Knock-knocka-knock-knock!
NOW WHO COULD THAT BE SO EARLY ON A SATURDAY MORNING?

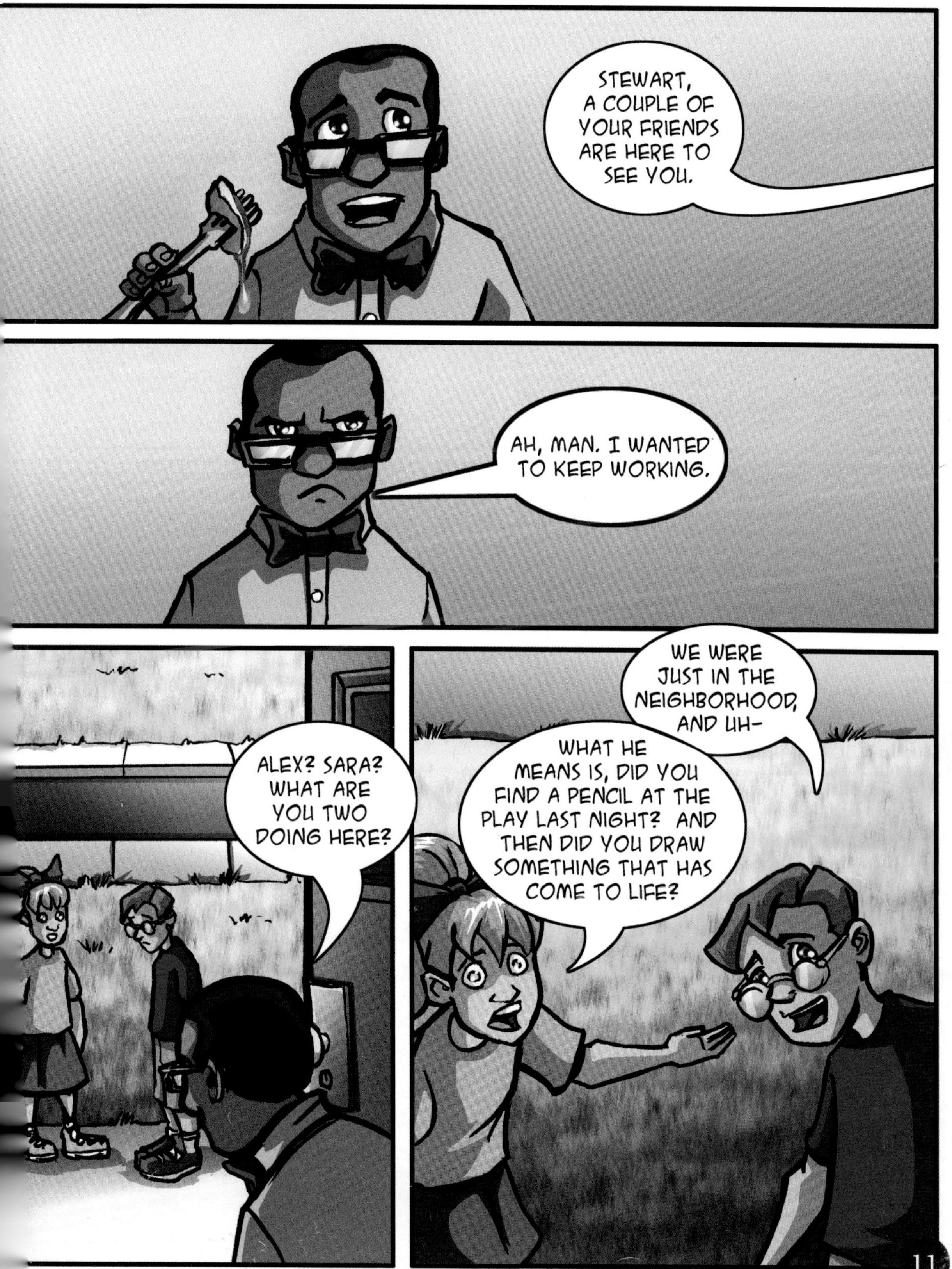
STEWART, A COUPLE OF YOUR FRIENDS ARE HERE TO SEE YOU.
AH, MAN. I WANTED TO KEEP WORKING.
ALEX? SARA? WHAT ARE YOU TWO DOING HERE?
WE WERE JUST IN THE NEIGHBORHOOD, AND UH-
WHAT HE MEANS IS, DID YOU FIND A PENCIL AT THE PLAY LAST NIGHT? AND THEN DID YOU DRAW SOMETHING THAT HAS COME TO LIFE?

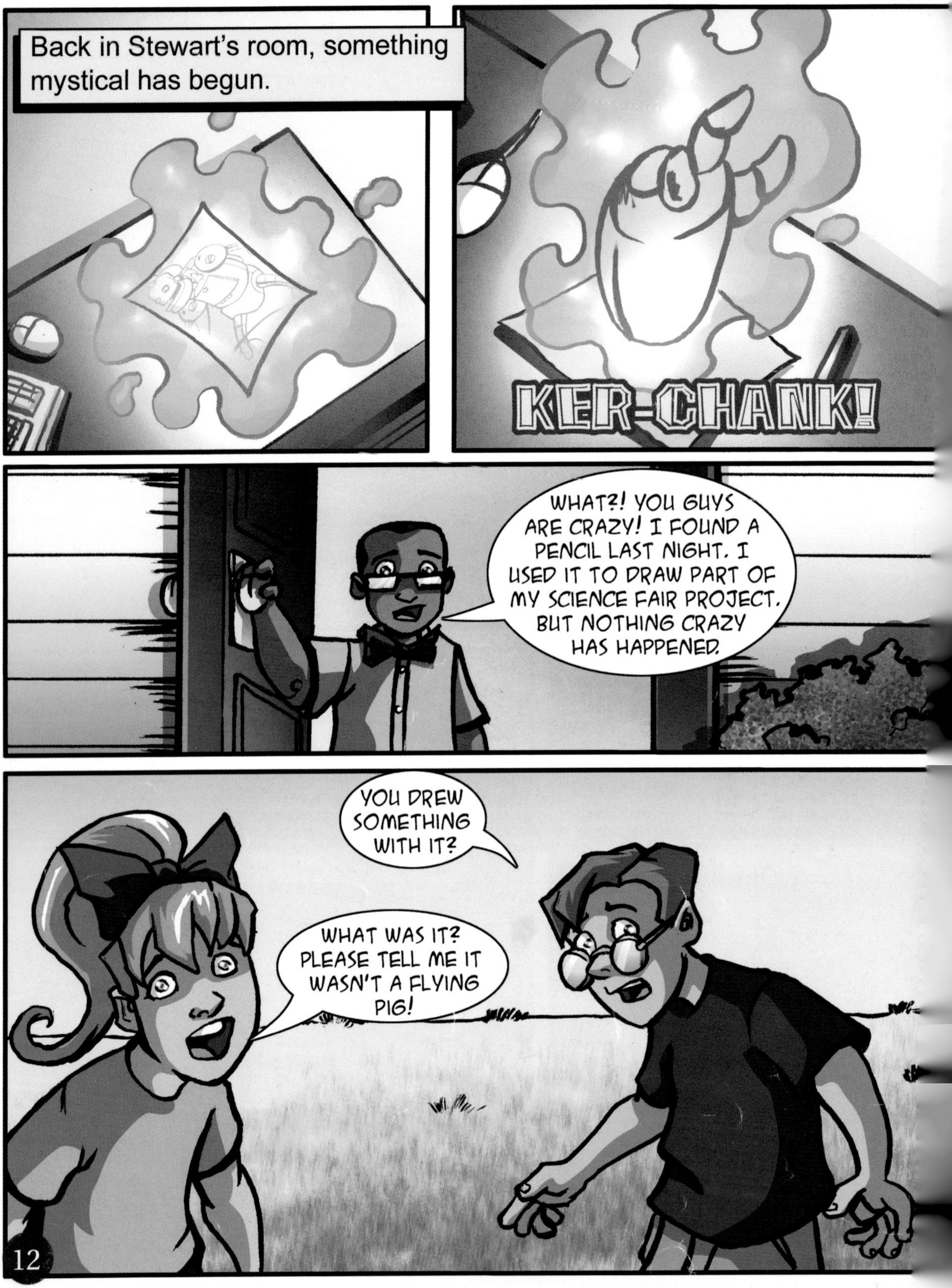

Back in Stewart's room, something mystical has begun.
KER-CHANK!
WHAT?! YOU GUYS ARE CRAZY! I FOUND A PENCIL LAST NIGHT. I USED IT TO DRAW PART OF MY SCIENCE FAIR PROJECT. BUT NOTHING CRAZY HAS HAPPENED.
YOU DREW SOMETHING WITH IT?
WHAT WAS IT? PLEASE TELL ME IT WASN'T A FLYING PIG!

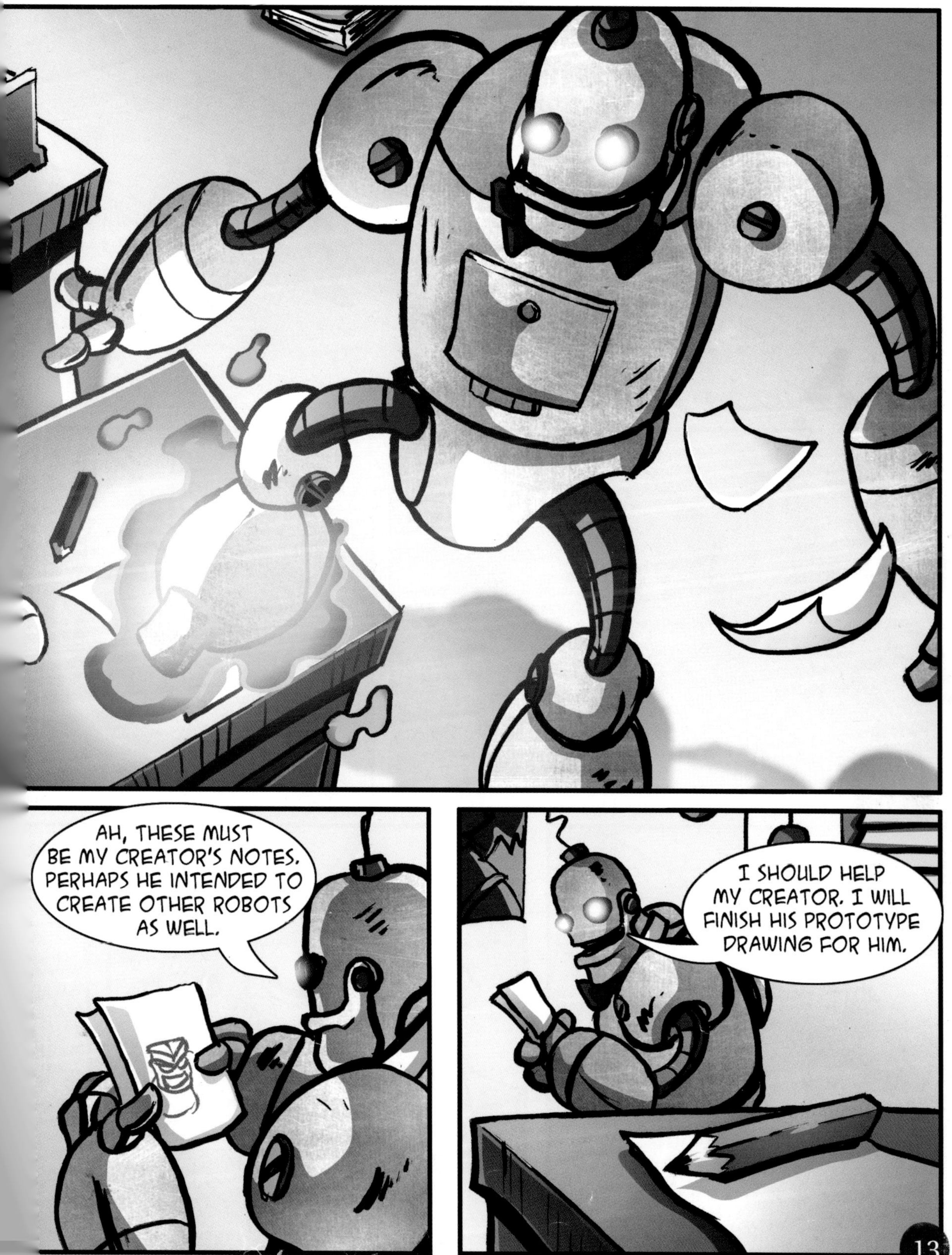
AH, THESE MUST BE MY CREATOR'S NOTES. PERHAPS HE INTENDED TO CREATE OTHER ROBOTS AS WELL.
I SHOULD HELP MY CREATOR. I WILL FINISH HIS PROTOTYPE DRAWING FOR HIM.

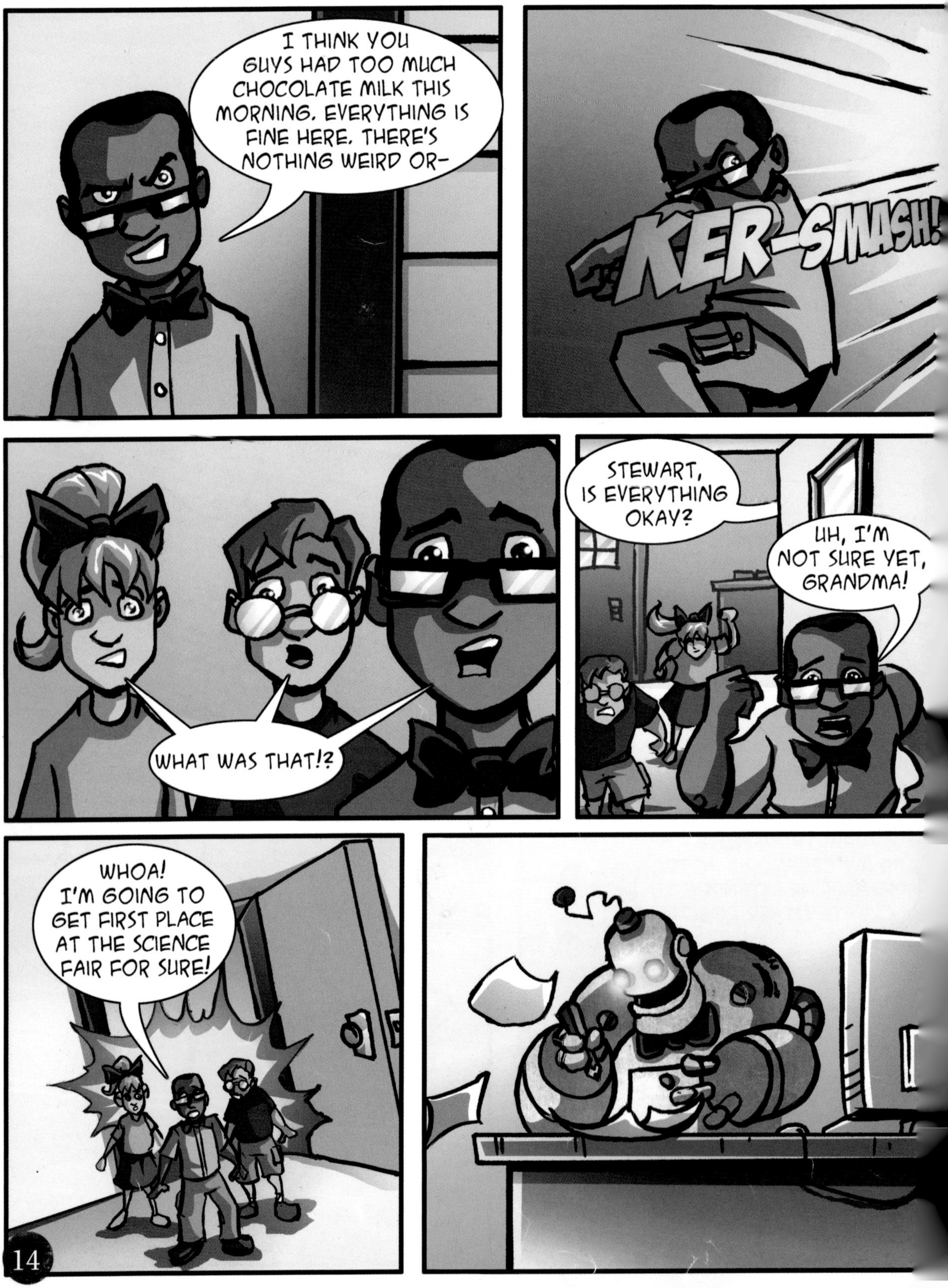

I THINK YOU GUYS HAD TOO MUCH CHOCOLATE MILK THIS MORNING. EVERYTHING IS FINE HERE. THERE'S NOTHING WEIRD OR-
KER-SMASH!
WHAT WAS THAT!?
STEWART, IS EVERYTHING OKAY?
UH, I'M NOT SURE YET, GRANDMA!
WHOA! I'M GOING TO GET FIRST PLACE AT THE SCIENCE FAIR FOR SURE!

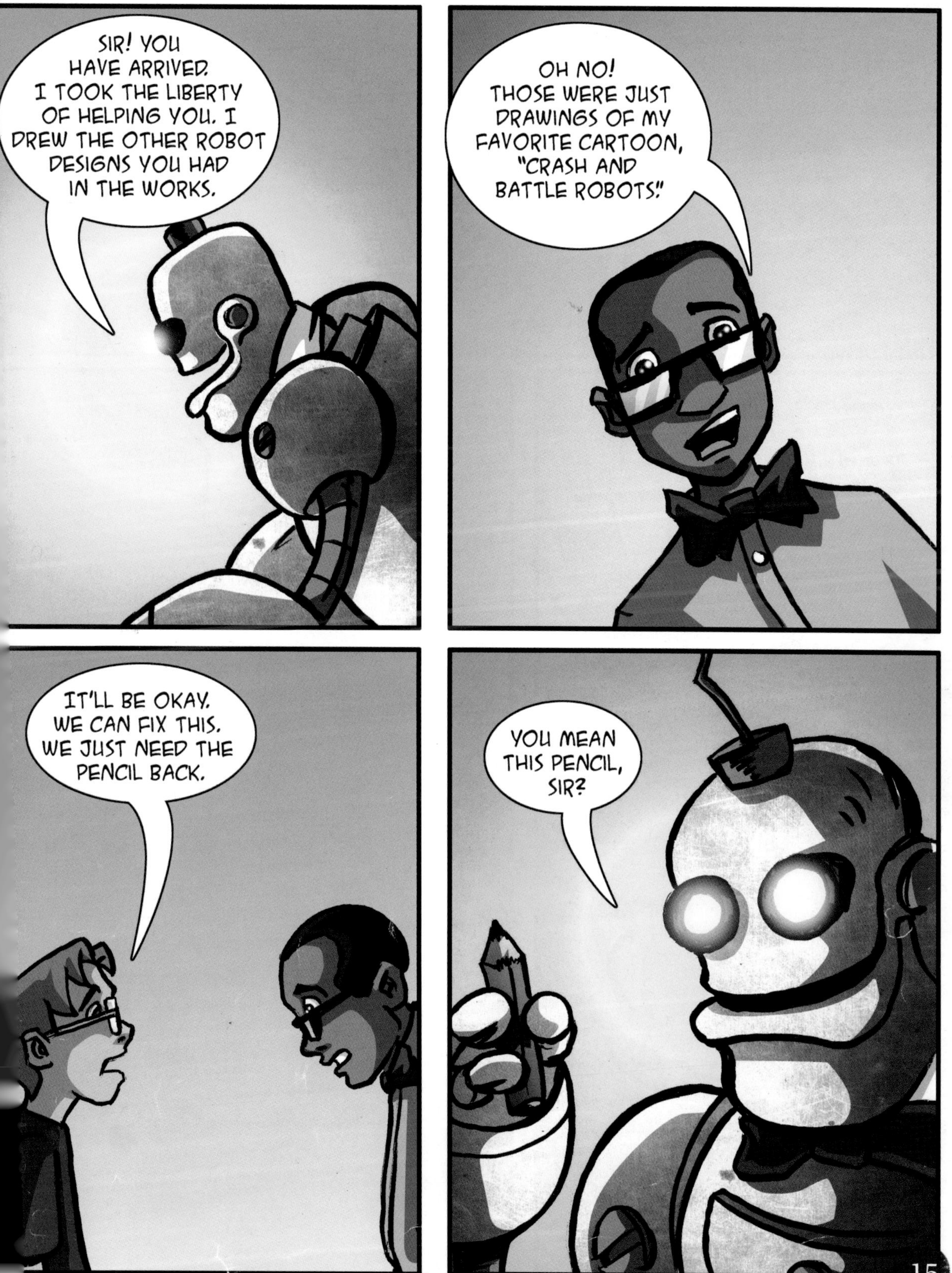
SIR! YOU HAVE ARRIVED. I TOOK THE LIBERTY OF HELPING YOU. I DREW THE OTHER ROBOT DESIGNS YOU HAD IN THE WORKS.
OH NO! THOSE WERE JUST DRAWINGS OF MY FAVORITE CARTOON, "CRASH AND BATTLE ROBOTS."
IT'LL BE OKAY. WE CAN FIX THIS. WE JUST NEED THE PENCIL BACK.
YOU MEAN THIS PENCIL, SIR?

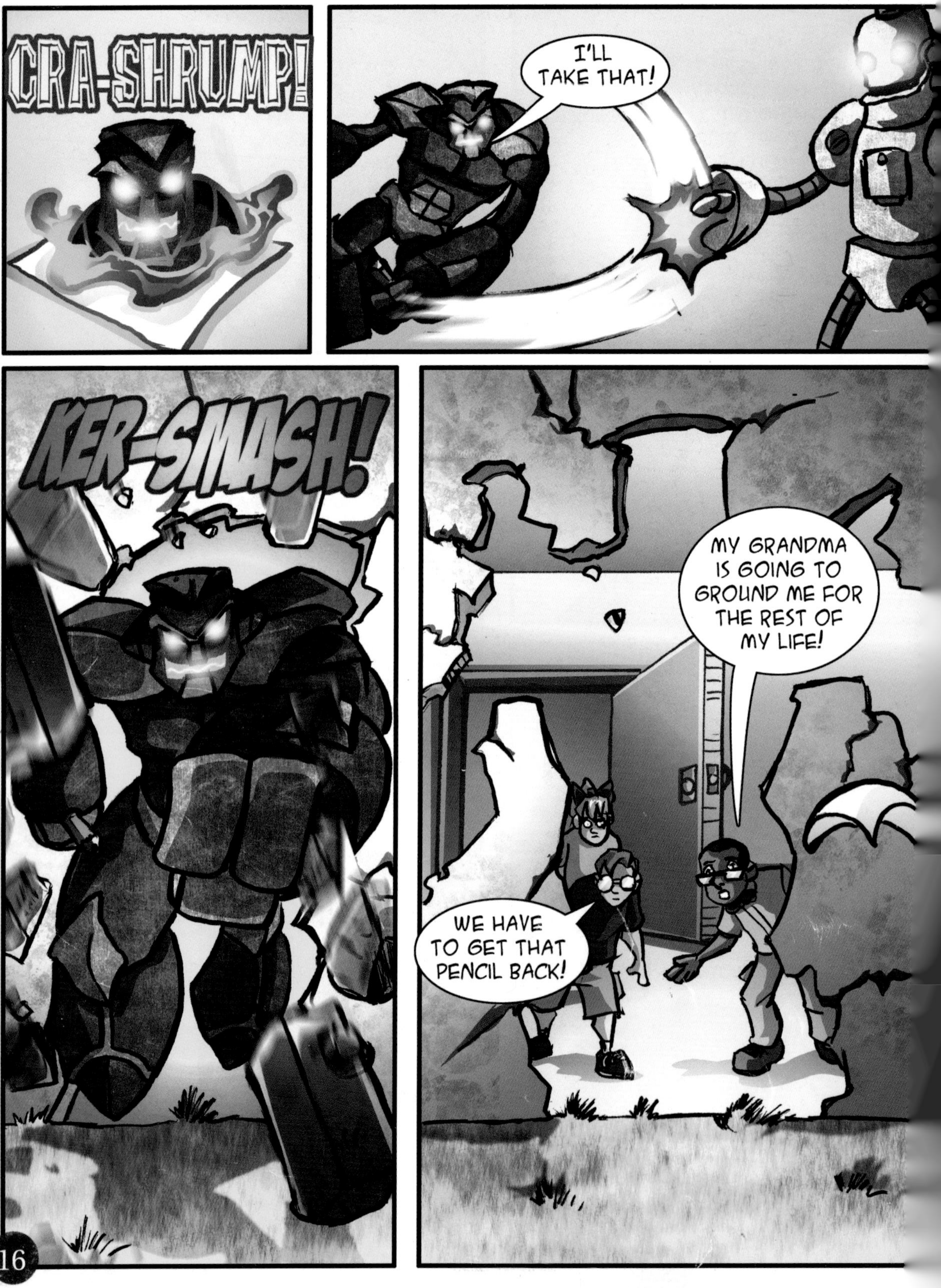
CRA-SHRUMP!
I'LL TAKE THAT!
KER-SMASH!
MY GRANDMA IS GOING TO GROUND ME FOR THE REST OF MY LIFE!
WE HAVE TO GET THAT PENCIL BACK!

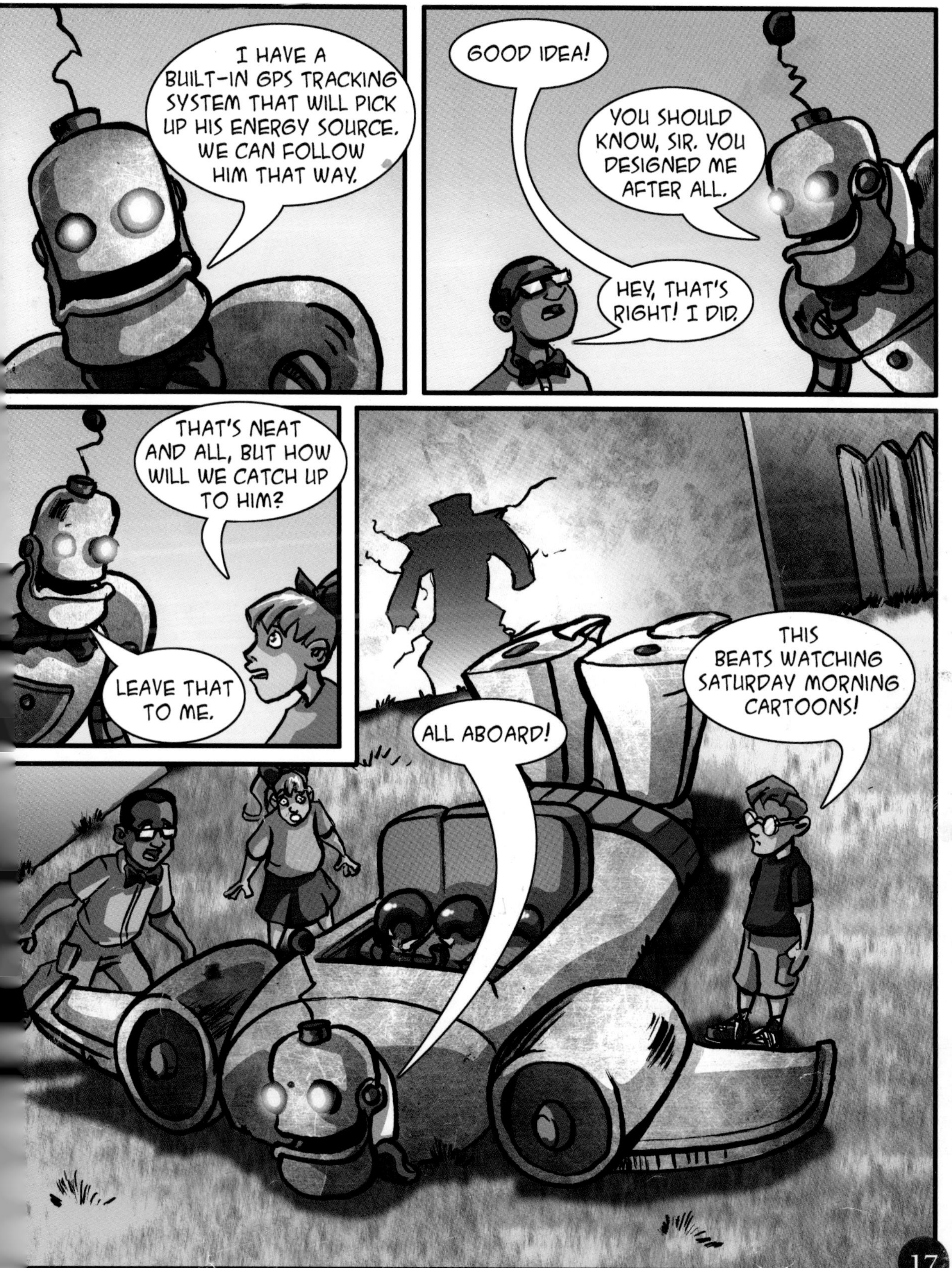
I HAVE A BUILT-IN GPS TRACKING SYSTEM THAT WILL PICK UP HIS ENERGY SOURCE. WE CAN FOLLOW HIM THAT WAY.
GOOD IDEA!
YOU SHOULD KNOW, SIR. YOU DESIGNED ME AFTER ALL.
HEY, THAT'S RIGHT! I DID.
THAT'S NEAT AND ALL, BUT HOW WILL WE CATCH UP TO HIM?
LEAVE THAT TO ME.
ALL ABOARD!
THIS BEATS WATCHING SATURDAY MORNING CARTOONS!

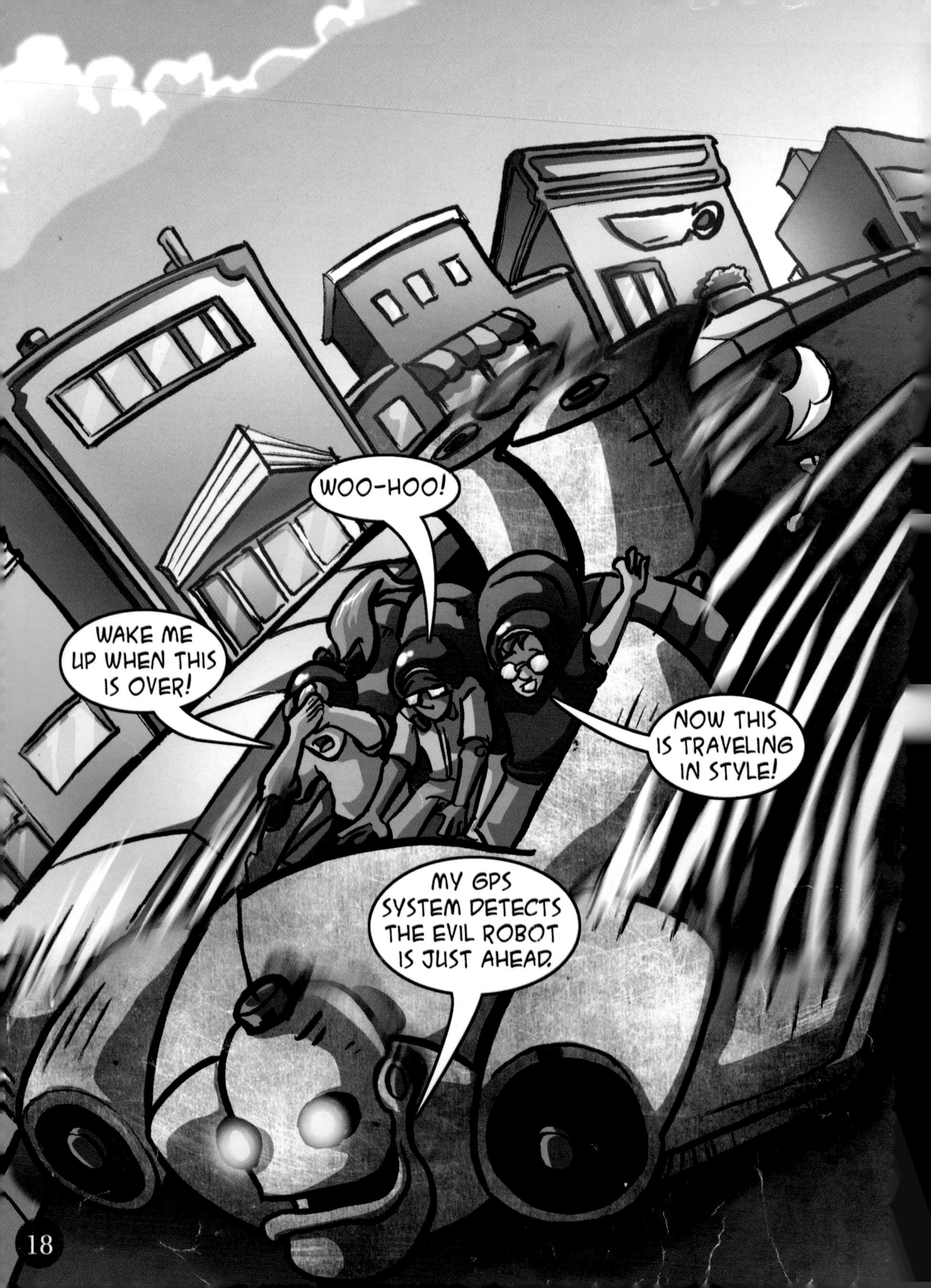
WOO-HOO!
WAKE ME UP WHEN THIS IS OVER!
NOW THIS IS TRAVELING IN STYLE!
MY GPS SYSTEM DETECTS THE EVIL ROBOT IS JUST AHEAD.

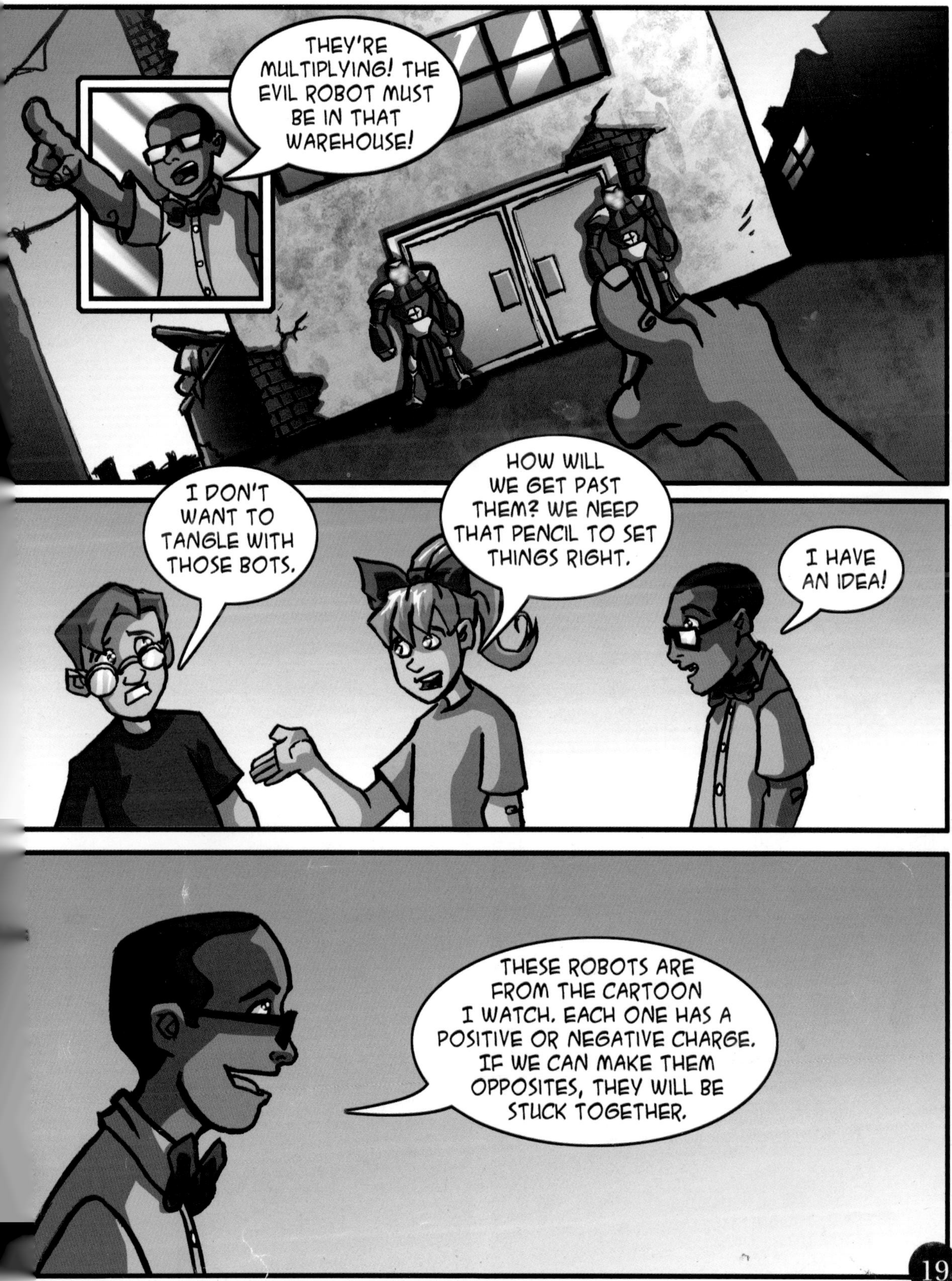
THEY'RE MULTIPLYING! THE EVIL ROBOT MUST BE IN THAT WAREHOUSE!
I DON'T WANT TO TANGLE WITH THOSE BOTS.
HOW WILL WE GET PAST THEM? WE NEED THAT PENCIL TO SET THINGS RIGHT.
I HAVE AN IDEA!
THESE ROBOTS ARE FROM THE CARTOON I WATCH. EACH ONE HAS A POSITIVE OR NEGATIVE CHARGE. IF WE CAN MAKE THEM OPPOSITES, THEY WILL BE STUCK TOGETHER.

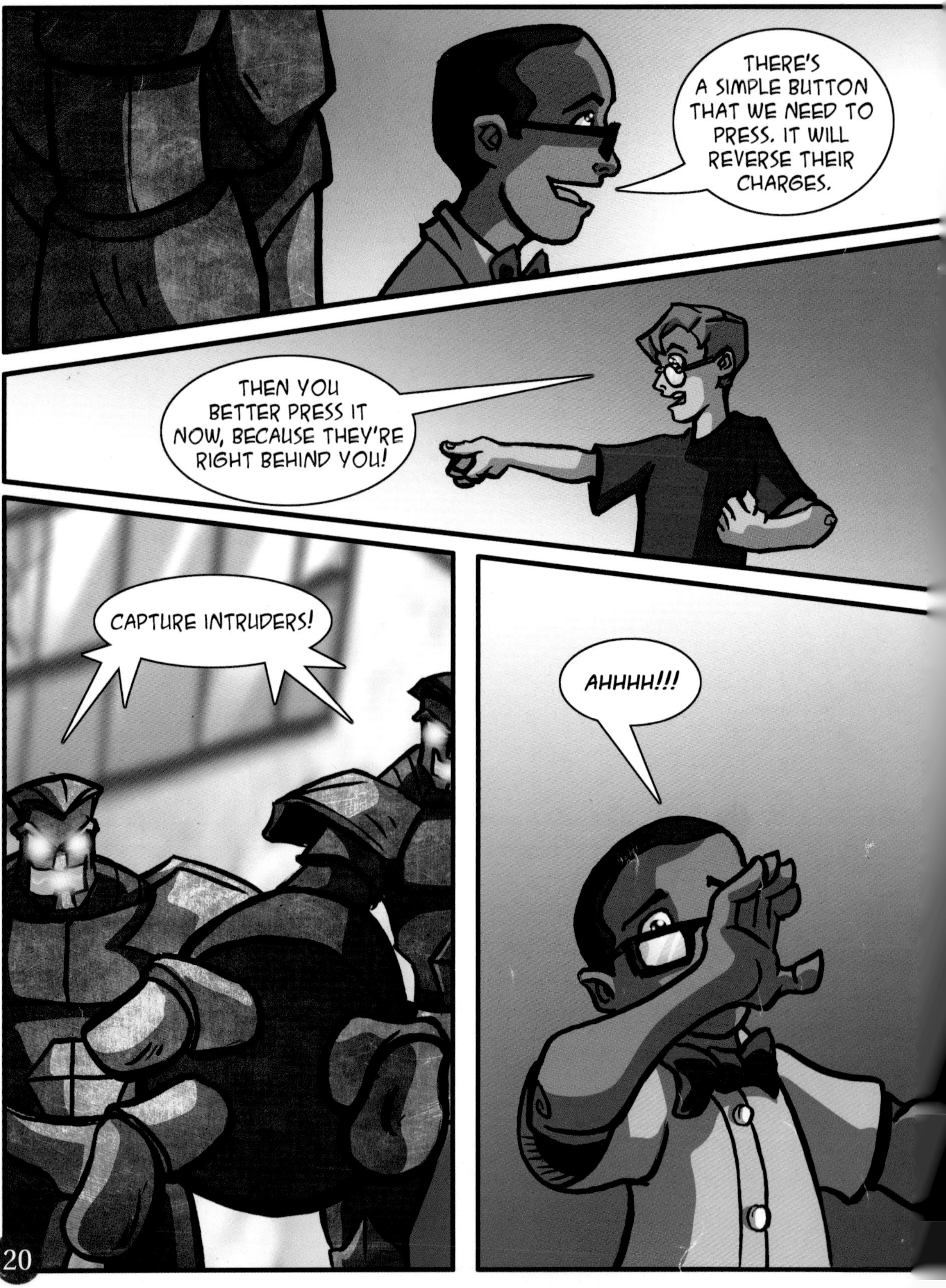
THERE'S A SIMPLE BUTTON THAT WE NEED TO PRESS. IT WILL REVERSE THEIR CHARGES.
THEN YOU BETTER PRESS IT NOW, BECAUSE THEY'RE RIGHT BEHIND YOU!
CAPTURE INTRUDERS!
AHHHH!!!

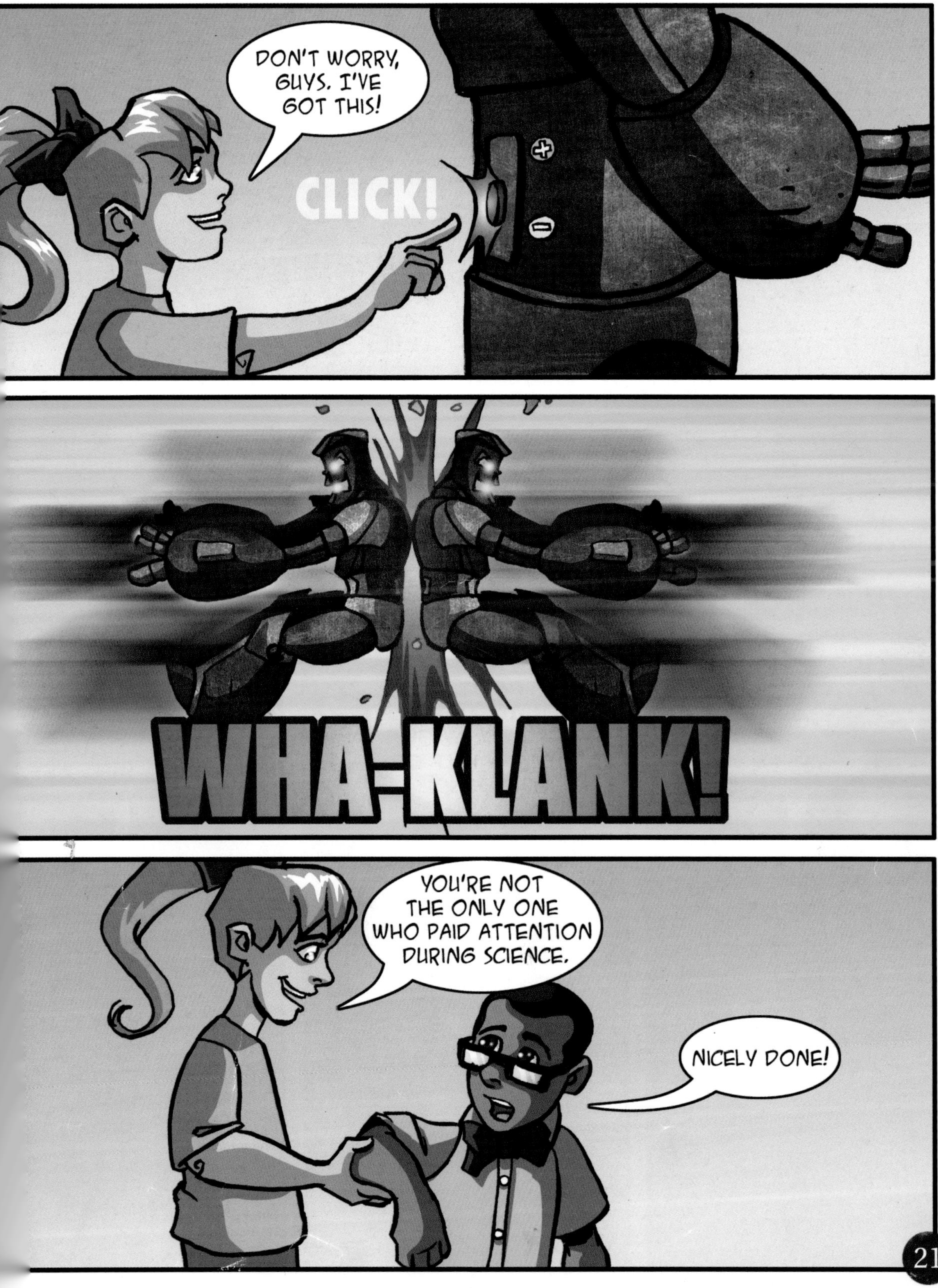
DON'T WORRY, GUYS. I'VE GOT THIS!
CLICK!
WHA-KLANK!
YOU'RE NOT THE ONLY ONE WHO PAID ATTENTION DURING SCIENCE.
NICELY DONE!

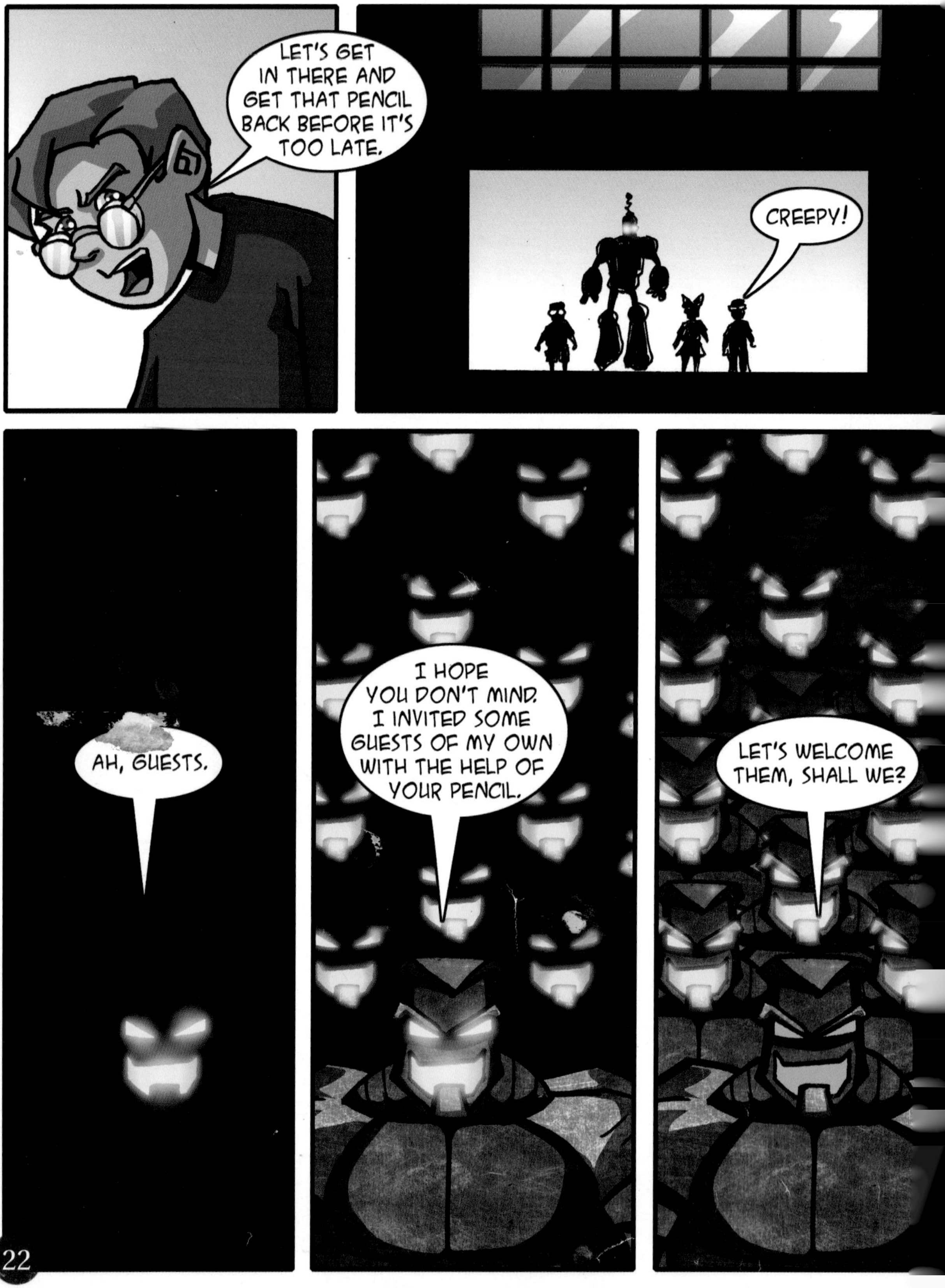
LET'S GET IN THERE AND GET THAT PENCIL BACK BEFORE IT'S TOO LATE.
CREEPY!
AH, GUESTS.
I HOPE YOU DON'T MIND. I INVITED SOME GUESTS OF MY OWN WITH THE HELP OF YOUR PENCIL.
LET'S WELCOME THEM, SHALL WE?

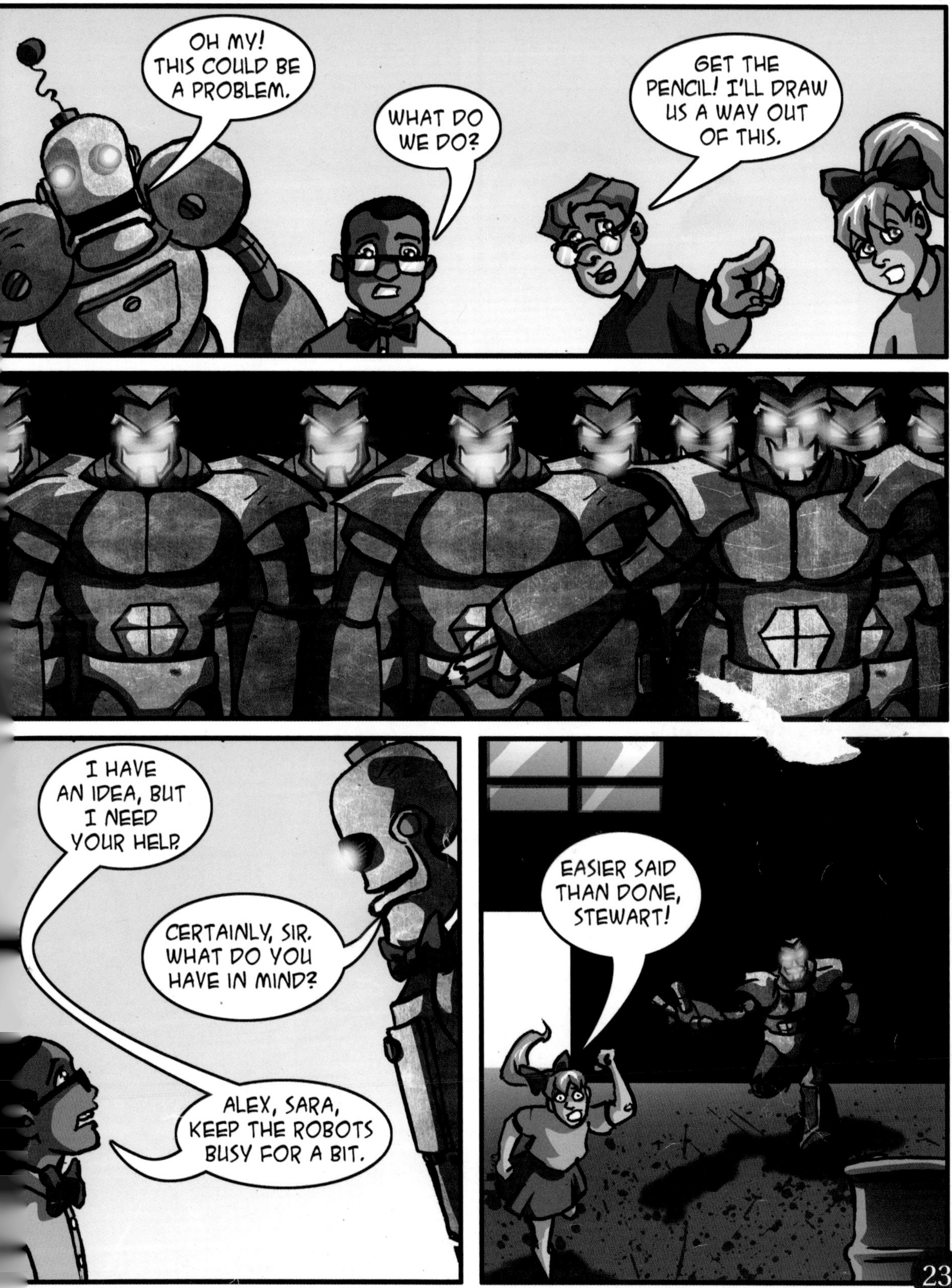
OH MY! THIS COULD BE A PROBLEM.
WHAT DO WE DO?
GET THE PENCIL! I'LL DRAW US A WAY OUT OF THIS.
I HAVE AN IDEA, BUT I NEED YOUR HELP.
CERTAINLY, SIR. WHAT DO YOU HAVE IN MIND?
ALEX, SARA, KEEP THE ROBOTS BUSY FOR A BIT.
EASIER SAID THAN DONE, STEWART!

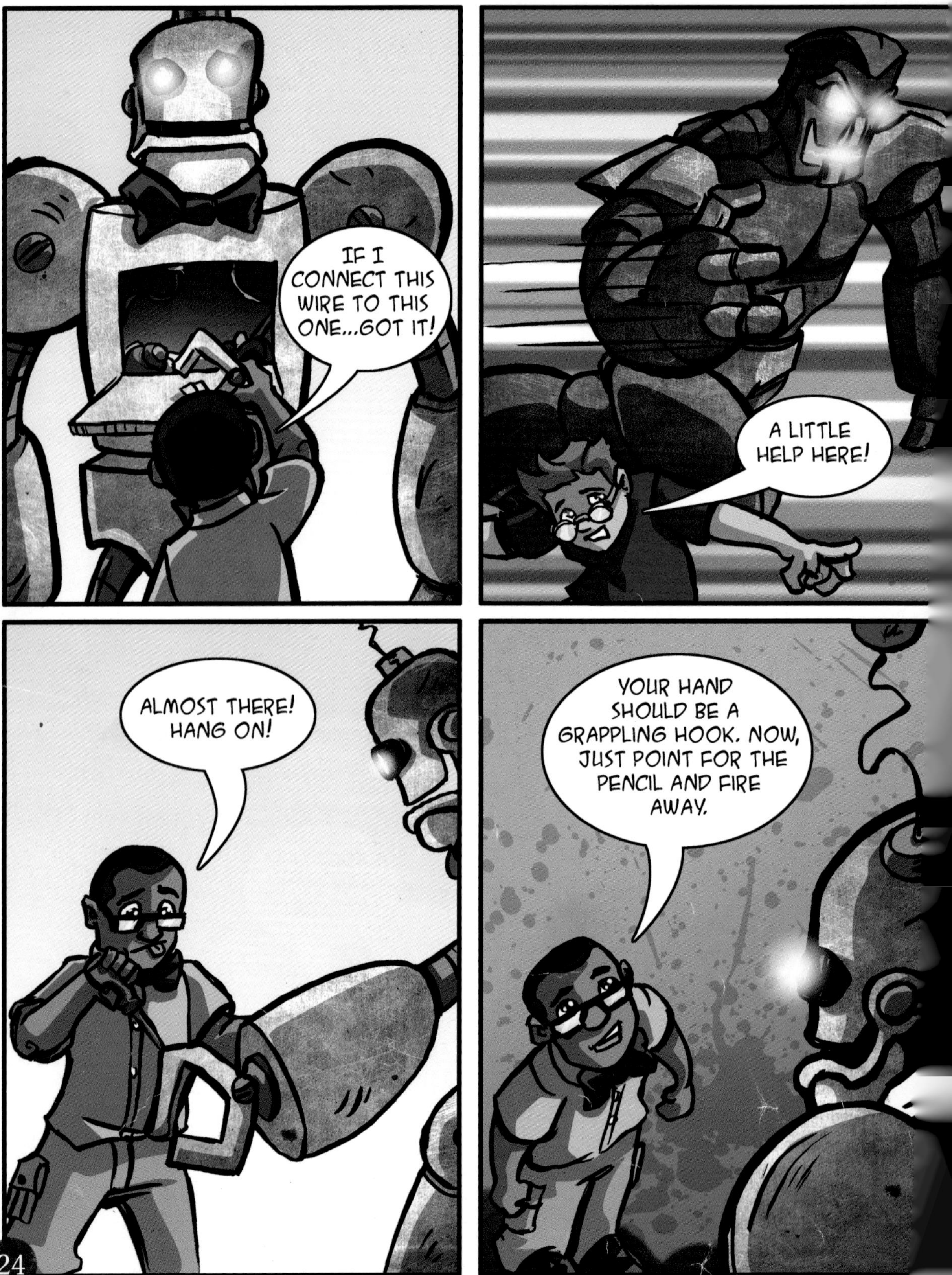
IF I CONNECT THIS WIRE TO THIS ONE...GOT IT!
A LITTLE HELP HERE!
ALMOST THERE! HANG ON!
YOUR HAND SHOULD BE A GRAPPLING HOOK. NOW, JUST POINT FOR THE PENCIL AND FIRE AWAY.

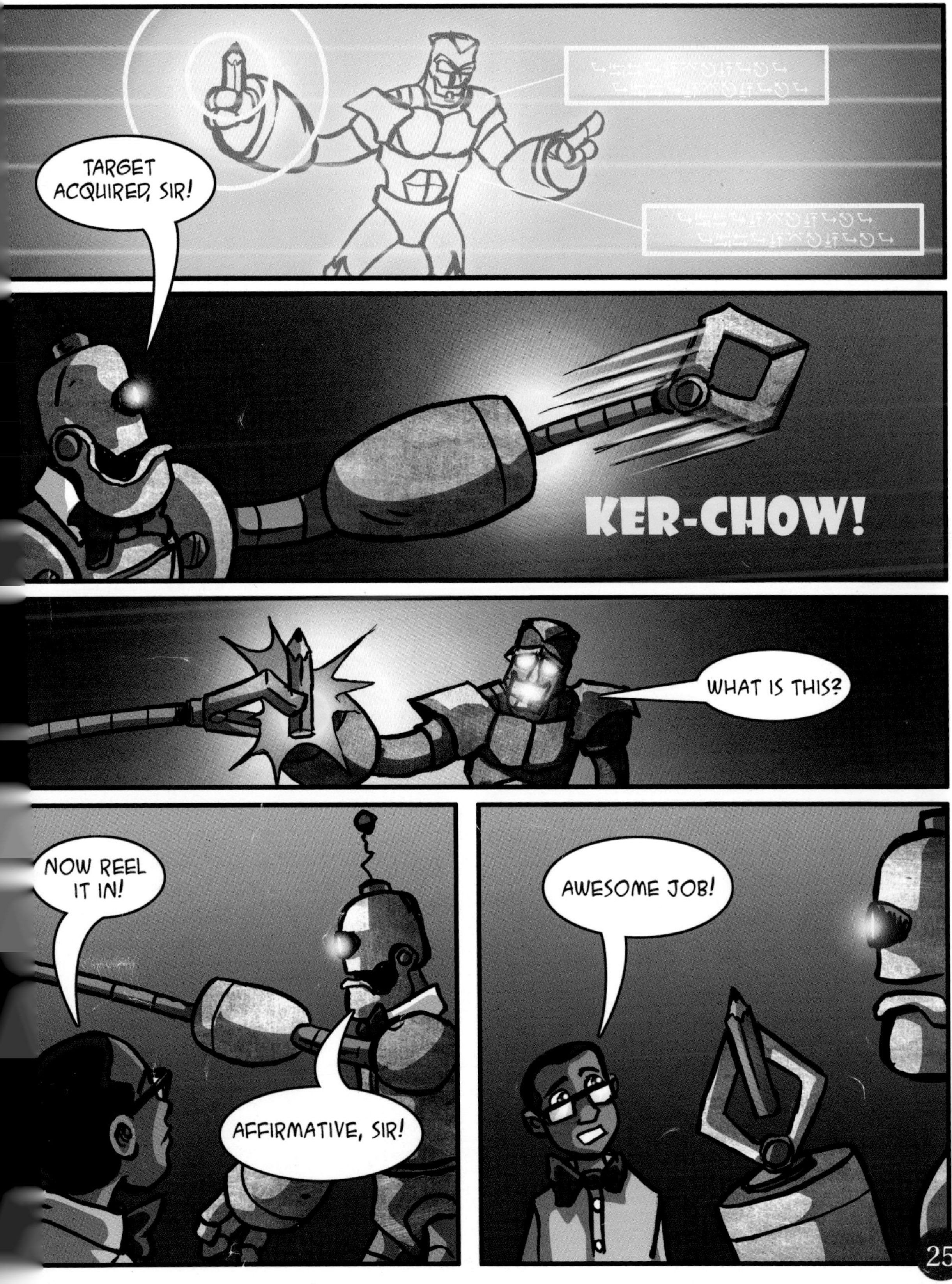
TARGET ACQUIRED, SIR!
KER-CHOW!
WHAT IS THIS?
NOW REEL IT IN!
AFFIRMATIVE, SIR!
AWESOME JOB!

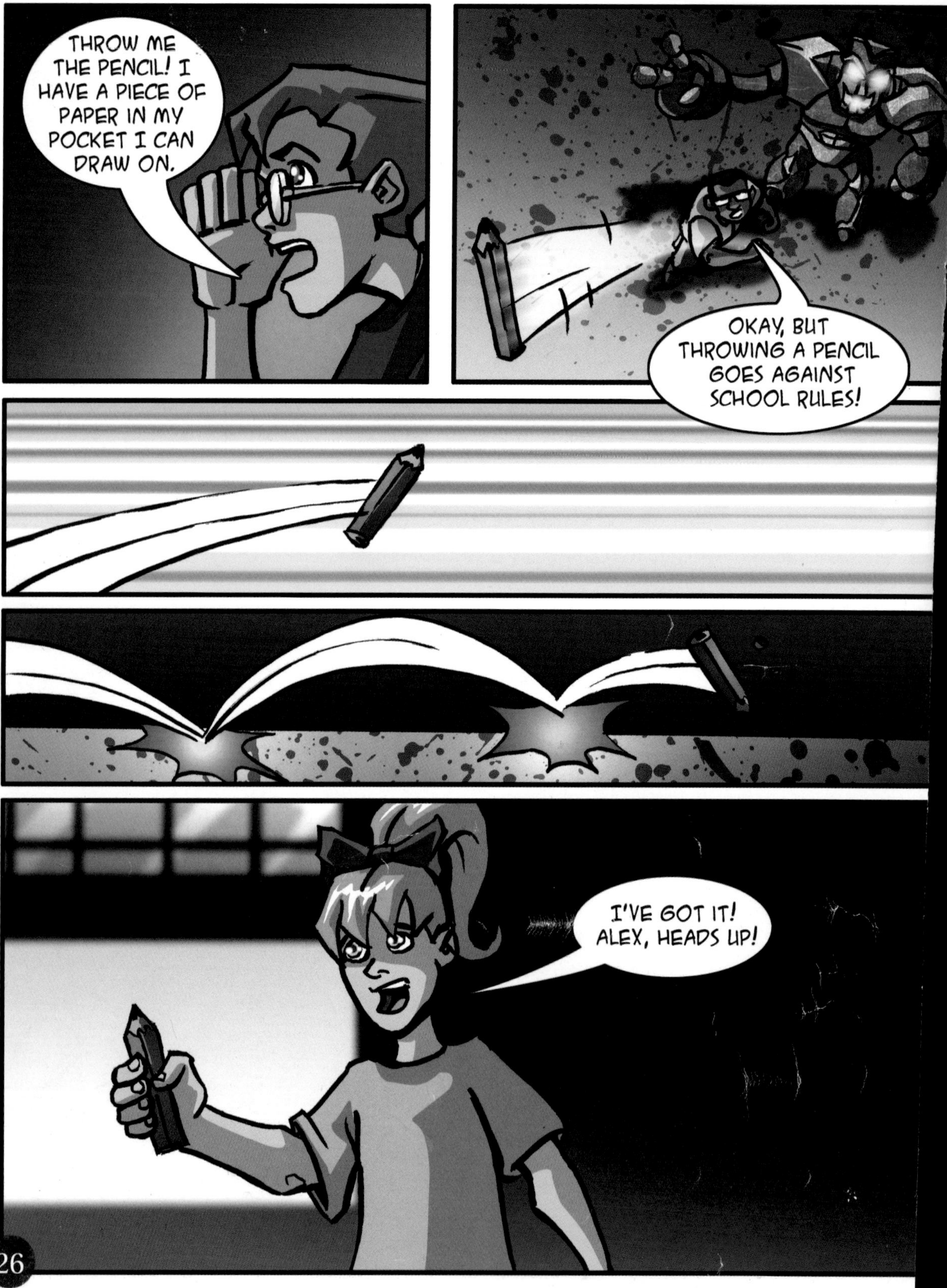
THROW ME THE PENCIL! I HAVE A PIECE OF PAPER IN MY POCKET I CAN DRAW ON.
OKAY, BUT THROWING A PENCIL GOES AGAINST SCHOOL RULES!
I'VE GOT IT! ALEX, HEADS UP!

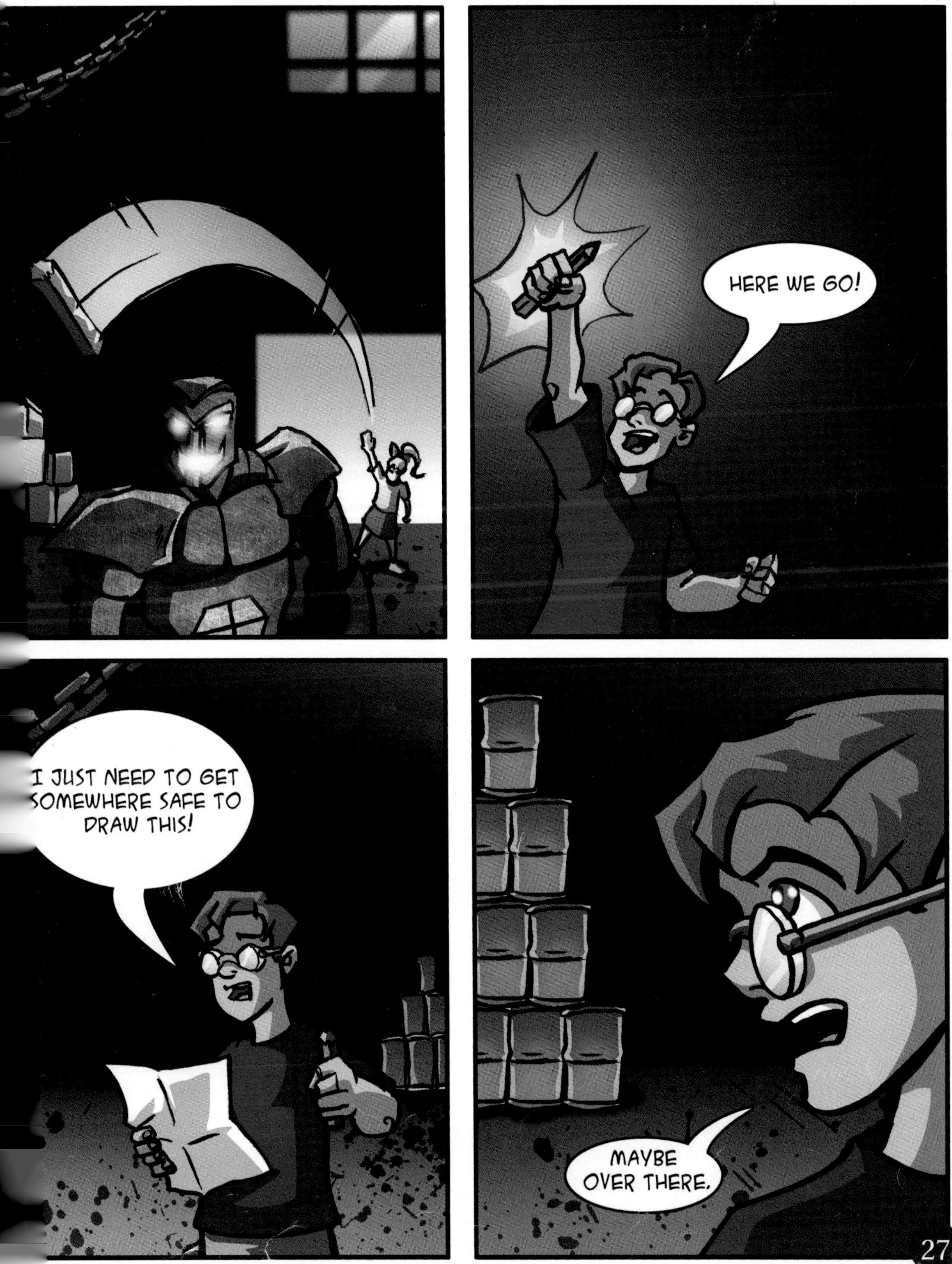
HERE WE GO!
I JUST NEED TO GET SOMEWHERE SAFE TO DRAW THIS!
MAYBE OVER THERE.

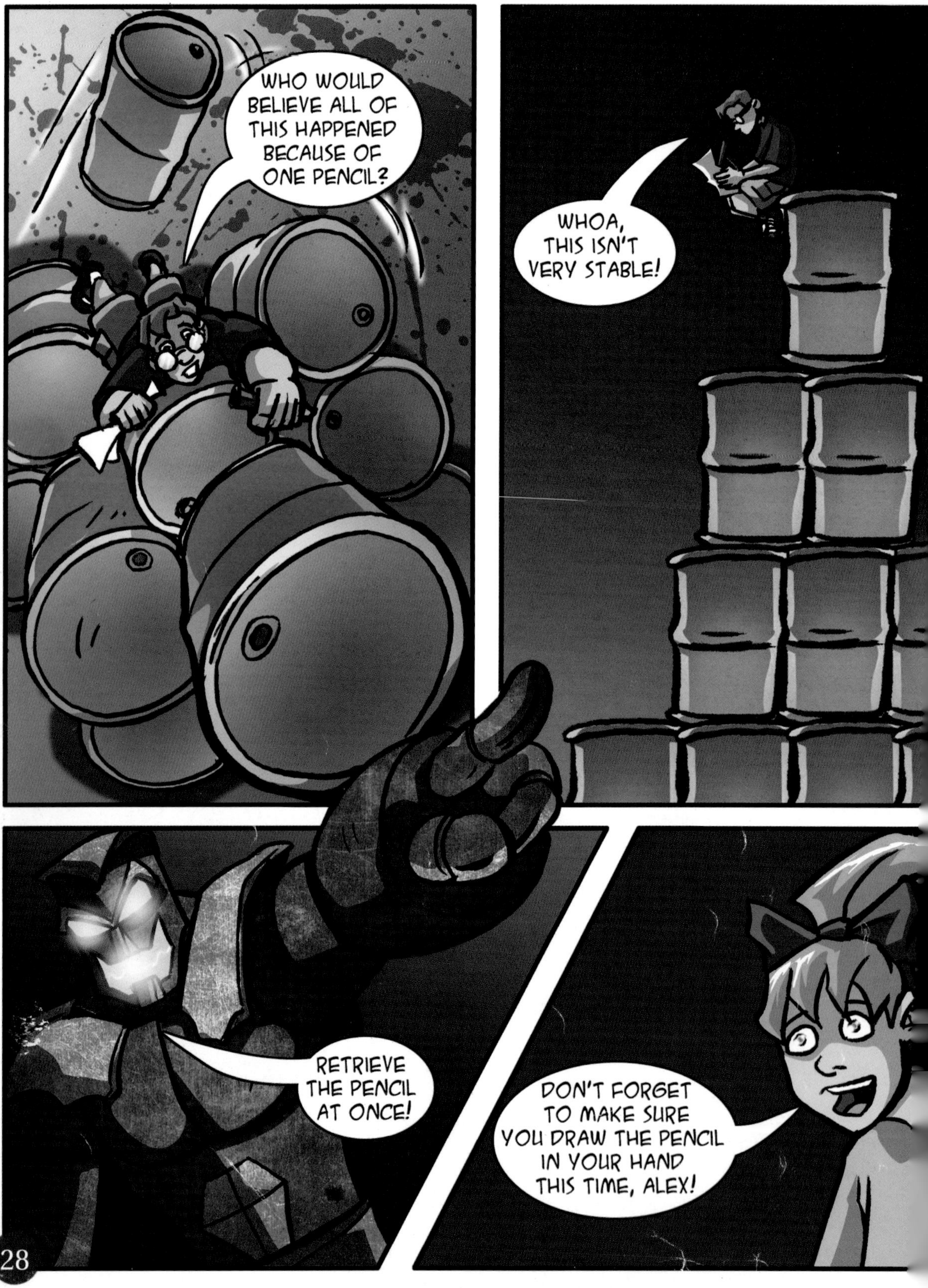
WHO WOULD BELIEVE ALL OF THIS HAPPENED BECAUSE OF ONE PENCIL?
WHOA, THIS ISN'T VERY STABLE!
RETRIEVE THE PENCIL AT ONCE!
DON'T FORGET TO MAKE SURE YOU DRAW THE PENCIL IN YOUR HAND THIS TIME, ALEX!

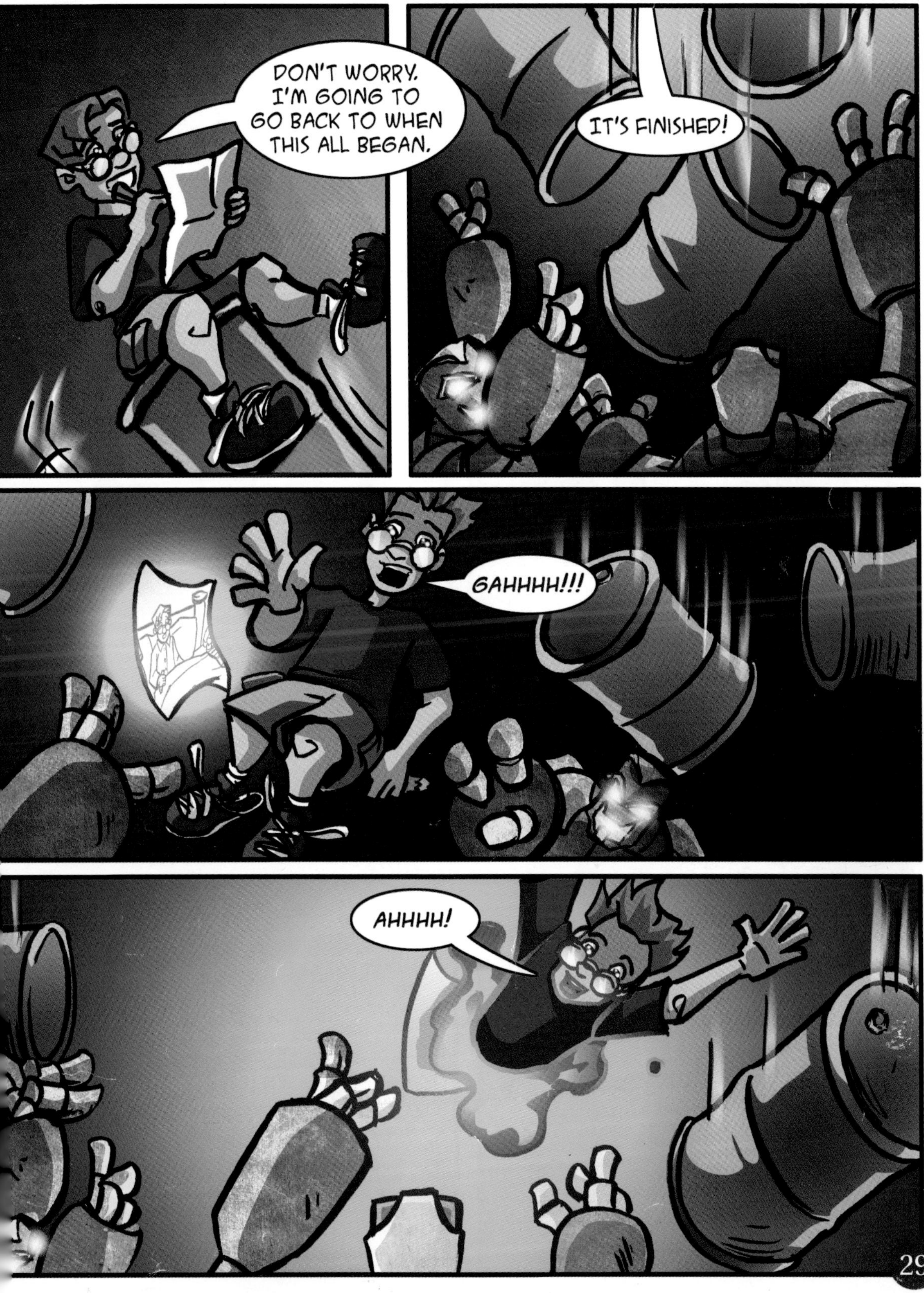
DON'T WORRY. I'M GOING TO GO BACK TO WHEN THIS ALL BEGAN.
IT'S FINISHED!
GAHHHH!!!
AHHHH!

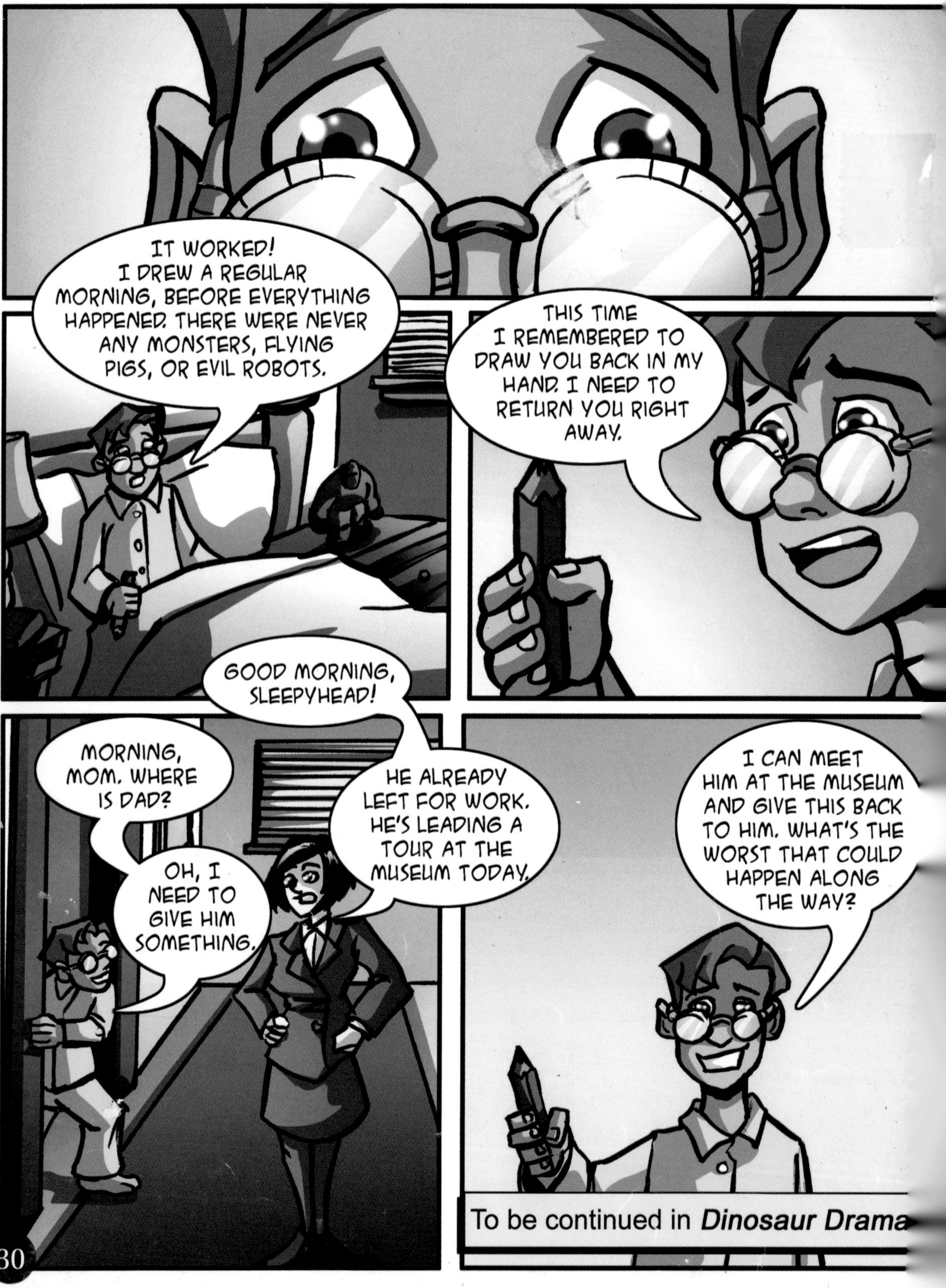
IT WORKED! I DREW A REGULAR MORNING, BEFORE EVERYTHING HAPPENED. THERE WERE NEVER ANY MONSTERS, FLYING PIGS, OR EVIL ROBOTS.
THIS TIME I REMEMBERED TO DRAW YOU BACK IN MY HAND. I NEED TO RETURN YOU RIGHT AWAY.
GOOD MORNING, SLEEPYHEAD!
MORNING, MOM. WHERE IS DAD?
HE ALREADY LEFT FOR WORK. HE'S LEADING A TOUR AT THE MUSEUM TODAY.
OH, I NEED TO GIVE HIM SOMETHING.
I CAN MEET HIM AT THE MUSEUM AND GIVE THIS BACK TO HIM. WHAT'S THE WORST THAT COULD HAPPEN ALONG THE WAY?
To be continued in *Dinosaur Drama*

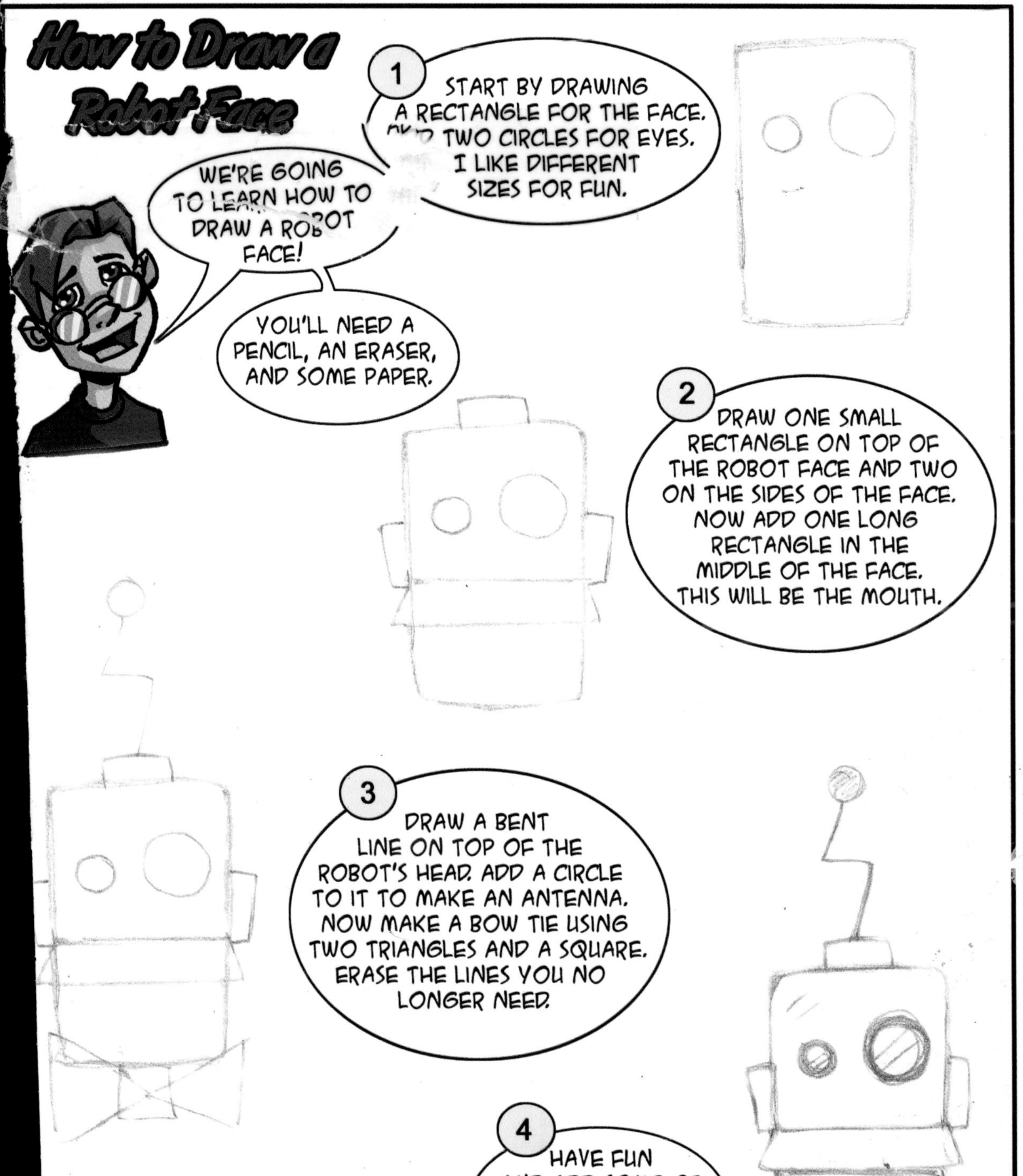
How to Draw a Robot Face
1
START BY DRAWING A RECTANGLE FOR THE FACE. AND TWO CIRCLES FOR EYES. I LIKE DIFFERENT SIZES FOR FUN.
WE'RE GOING TO LEARN HOW TO DRAW A ROBOT FACE!
YOU'LL NEED A PENCIL, AN ERASER, AND SOME PAPER.
2
DRAW ONE SMALL RECTANGLE ON TOP OF THE ROBOT FACE AND TWO ON THE SIDES OF THE FACE. NOW ADD ONE LONG RECTANGLE IN THE MIDDLE OF THE FACE. THIS WILL BE THE MOUTH.
3
DRAW A BENT LINE ON TOP OF THE ROBOT'S HEAD. ADD A CIRCLE TO IT TO MAKE AN ANTENNA. NOW MAKE A BOW TIE USING TWO TRIANGLES AND A SQUARE. ERASE THE LINES YOU NO LONGER NEED.
4
HAVE FUN AND ADD SOME OF YOUR OWN IDEAS. DON'T FORGET TO PRACTICE!

About the Author

Dustin Evans was born and raised in Oklahoma. In 2005, Dustin graduated from Oklahoma State University with a BFA in Graphic Design & Illustration. He has since gone on to work with such companies as Disney, IDW Publishing, Magic Wagon, and more. His work can be seen in comic books and children's books and on apparel and TV. He enjoys spending time with his family and pets, reading, drawing, and going to museums and movies.

Dustin begins each page with simple pencil and paper. Working from the script, he creates a rough layout for each page. Once the layouts are ready, he then scans the images into the computer to make them larger. The next step is to print out the larger layout, transfer it to the final page using a light box, and then ink the final image. Dustin then goes back to the computer to scan the final, inked image. Now it's time to add digital color, special effects, and lettering using computer programs. Finally, the image is complete and ready for print after some fine-tuning with any needed edits.

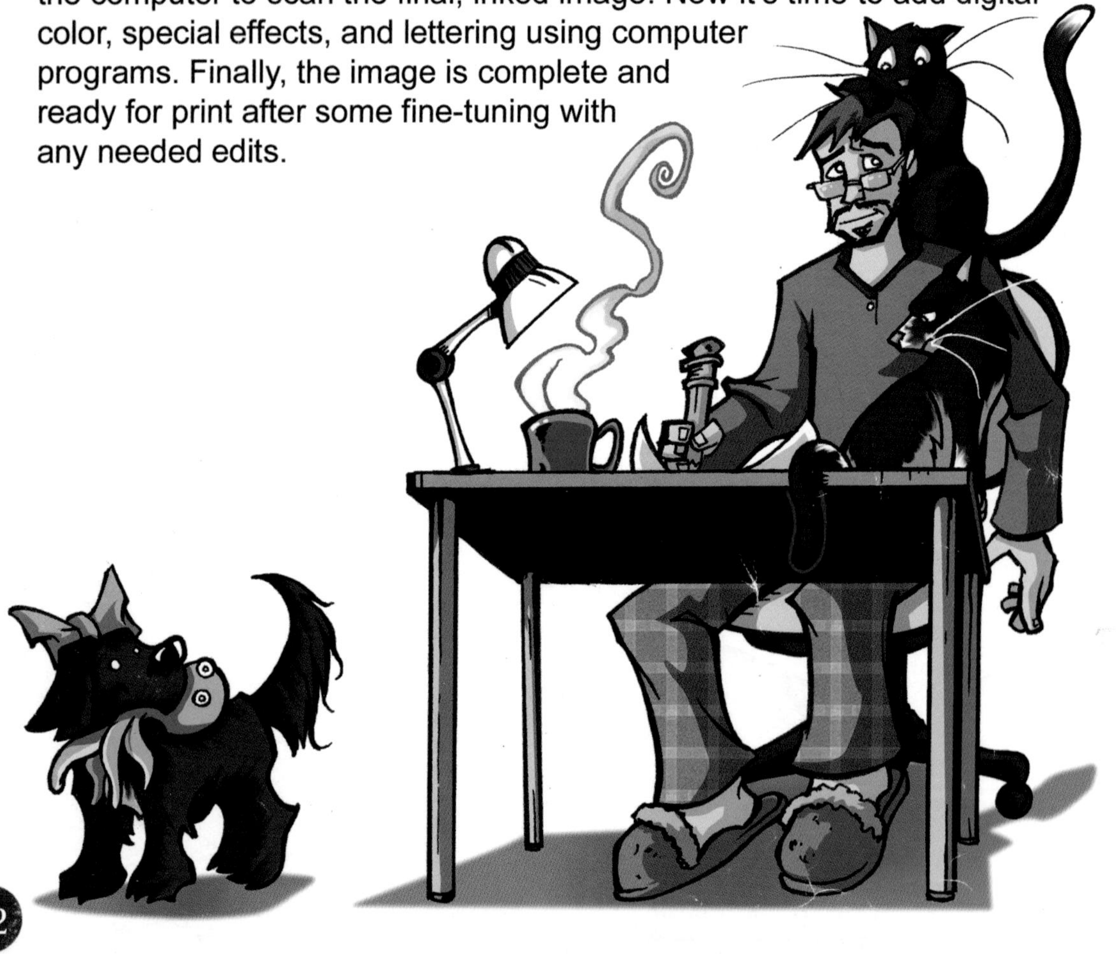